An Amish Christmas Journey

Patricia Davids

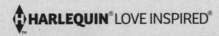

Recycling programs
for this product may
not exist in your area.

™ LOVE INSPIRED BOOKS

ISBN-13: 978-0-373-87927-4

An Amish Christmas Journey

www.Harlequin.com

Printed in U.S.A.

"Do you do that often?" Greta asked.

He opened his eyes and frowned. "Do I do what?"

"Refuse help when you need it?"

He gave her a wry smile. "Am I guilty of being prideful? I have been, but I'm learning that I can't do everything."

Greta gathered her things. "Then stretch out on this bench and take a nap. I will keep an eye on your sister and wake you if she needs anything."

He nodded his consent. Greta moved up to one of the single seats where she could keep an eye on Marianne and on Toby. He folded his long legs on the seat and pillowed his head on his coat. It wasn't long before his breathing became deep and even and she knew he was asleep.

She had never watched a man sleeping before. At least no one younger than the elders who sometimes nodded off during the long church services.

At leisure to study him, Greta assessed his features one by one, trying to decide why she was so attracted to him.

The lines of strain around Toby's eyes touched a chord within her. She wanted to see them soothed away.

Books by Patricia Davids

Love Inspired

His Bundle of Love
Love Thine Enemy
Prodigal Daughter
The Color of Courage
Military Daddy
A Matter of the Heart
A Military Match
A Family for Thanksgiving
*Katie's Redemption
*The Doctor's Blessing
*An Amish Christmas
*The Farmer Next Door
*The Christmas Quilt
*A Home for Hannah
*A Hope Springs Christmas
*Plain Admirer
*Amish Christmas Joy
*The Shepherd's Bride
*The Amish Nanny
*An Amish Christmas Journey

*Brides of Amish Country

Love Inspired Suspense

A Cloud of Suspicion
Speed Trap

PATRICIA DAVIDS

After thirty-five years as a nurse, Pat hung up her stethoscope to become a full-time writer. She enjoys spending her new free time visiting her grandchildren, doing some long-overdue yard work and traveling to research her story locations. She resides in Wichita, Kansas. Pat always enjoys hearing from her readers. You can visit her online at www.patriciadavids.com.

If thou, Lord, shouldest mark iniquities,
O Lord, who shall stand?
But there is forgiveness with thee,
that thou mayest be feared.
I wait for the Lord, my soul doth wait,
and in his word do I hope.
—*Psalms* 130:3–5

This book is dedicated to women and men
everywhere who seek to mend fences and to
right wrongs within their families.

Blessed are the peacemakers:
for they shall be called the children of God.
—*Matthew* 5:9

Chapter One

"I suppose we must do it." Greta Barkman almost choked on her words.

It was the right thing to say. The only decision her Amish faith would let her make, but she'd rather walk through the snow barefoot…all winter…than spend one hour with her uncle Morris. Bringing him home to stay with them for a few months would be unbearable. Surely God would not ask this of her and her sisters after all they had endured.

Betsy, the youngest at eighteen, slapped the letter face-down on the table. "It's not as if *Onkel* Morris can expect us to drop everything and rush to his side. We escaped his cruelness by the grace of God. Besides, it's almost Christmas. It will be our first happy Christmas together. I don't want him to spoil it."

He will spoil it. I know that as surely as I know it's cold outside.

Greta glanced at the kitchen window. The late-afternoon sun shone brightly beyond the frost-covered glass, but it added little warmth to the December day. The dusting of snow that had arrived in the night blew around, sparkling like glitter in the breeze. She shivered and looked back at the people seated around her grandfather's table. Her three sisters, her grandfather and his new wife, and two of her sisters' husbands were gathered for this family meeting.

Clara, the oldest sister, picked up the letter. "I agree with Greta. We have to do this. His bishop would not write asking us to take Morris in if our uncle's condition were not serious." She glanced at her husband seated beside her. "I will go, if you agree, Ethan."

He covered her hand with his own. "I won't pretend that I like the idea, but you must do what you think best. The children and I will manage without you for a few days."

"I can go." Lizzie, the second sister, looked as though she would rather eat dirt.

Carl, Lizzie's husband, laid his hand on her arm. "I won't agree to it. You have to think of the babe. Such a long car ride will not be good for you."

Naomi, their grandfather's wife, reached over to clasp Lizzie's hand. "You know the midwife cautioned against traveling with the problems you've had."

Lizzie nodded in resignation, but Greta detected a hint of relief in her eyes. Who could blame her?

Greta retrieved the letter and scanned it again. Their uncle lived near Fort Wayne, Indiana. She explained the contents for those that hadn't read it. "His bishop writes that the congregation is willing to arrange for a van and driver to take Morris from the hospital to our home. His doctors wouldn't allow him to travel by bus. A car or van is acceptable as long as the driver makes frequent stops. Morris must take brief walks every hour or two to prevent circulation problems with his legs."

And he must have someone travel with him. The five-hour car trip from Fort Wayne to Hope Springs would need to be broken into at least two days of travel. It would make a very long trip, breaks or no breaks.

Although the bishop hinted at some dissention among his flock over the matter, the fact that none of them were willing to take Morris in spoke of a serious rift in the church group. The Amish took care of their own within the community. Families were expected to look after aging or ailing members and normally did so gladly. His nieces were all the family Morris Barkman had left.

Lizzie crossed her arms over her chest. "I can't believe old man Rufus turned Morris out of the house and hired a new fellow to work the dairy farm. I thought our *onkel* and his landlord were friends."

"I can believe it," Clara said with a shiver. "Rufus Kuhns is an evil man. He's worse than our uncle."

Greta nodded in agreement. Rufus had tried to coerce Clara into marrying him by threatening all of them with eviction and physical violence. "Morris is out of a job and has nowhere to live. He is dependent on us, the very women he mistreated for years. It must be a bitter pill for him."

It was for her. For all of them.

Naomi sighed heavily. "Greta, you are the only logical choice to go and fetch him here."

She looked up startled. "Me? Why me?"

Naomi's gaze softened with sympathy. "Lizzie can't go. Betsy has a job and shouldn't miss work, besides she is too young to travel so far alone. Clara is a newlywed. She has a new husband and three stepchildren to think about. It would be cruel to part her from the children so soon. I'm not related to Morris. He might find it uncomfortable traveling with me."

"I don't care if he is comfortable or not!" Greta couldn't do it. She couldn't spend two days shut in a car with him.

"I don't know how I would manage without you for even a day, Naomi." Joseph reached to take his new wife's hand.

Greta saw the warm look he exchanged with Naomi. It seemed everyone in her family had found someone to love. Everyone but her. Betsy was being courted by a local Amish fellow that everyone liked. Lizzie had married Carl last fall, and they were expecting their first child. Clara had wed Ethan Gingerich only a few weeks ago.

Greta had refused the few men who had asked her out. Marriage wasn't in her future, certainly not marriage to an Amish man. She wanted to become a counselor and help abused women. To do that would require more education than the eight years the Amish allowed. Leaving the community she loved was a difficult decision—one she wasn't sure she was ready to make. She had only discussed it with Clara. No one else knew what she was thinking of doing.

Greta didn't begrudge any of her sisters their happiness. They deserved it and more. How many times had her actions and her words brought their uncle's wrath down on them? Far more that she cared to count. If only she had been stronger. If only she had stood up to him. If only she had told someone about the abuse, but she hadn't. They had all lived inside a circle of fear and shame until Lizzie found the courage to break out. It was because of Lizzie that they found a refuge of love and caring in their grandfather's home. God had rewarded Lizzie's selfless bravery.

Greta didn't possess such courage. The thought of spending time with Morris made her cringe. She couldn't do it. Panic hit her full in the face. She crumpled the letter and jumped to her feet. "Someone else will have to go."

She ran out of the room and up the stairs with her heart hammering wildly in her chest. She was staring out her bedroom window struggling to regain her composure when Naomi came in. Without turning around, Greta said, "I can't do it."

Naomi slipped an arm across Greta's shoulders. "Betsy has said she will go."

Greta flinched. Her little sister was no match for Morris. "Betsy is too young. He's too mean. You don't know how he is. He can make her feel worthless with nothing but words. He doesn't even need his stick to beat her down."

"I'm not saying it will be easy for her, but she's willing to do it to spare you."

Greta bit the corner of her lip. "I'm afraid, Naomi."

"Of what, child?"

"That I'll turn back into the groveling, miserable person I was when I lived with him. He called me Mouse because I was always scurrying out of his path. I existed—I didn't live. I was dead inside."

She still was. In spite of all she had read about surviving abuse, she knew Morris still had a hold over her. "I don't have Lizzie's courage."

Naomi enfolded her in a fierce hug. "Courage is fear that has said its prayers. God will give you all you need if you depend on Him."

Drawing strength from the woman she had come to love and admire, Greta nodded. Now it was her turn to be brave. To prove to herself and to him that she wasn't worthless. "All right, I will go."

Naomi pulled away to look into Greta's eyes. "Are you sure?"

She would be coolly polite. She would ignore her uncle's hurtful ways, and she would never, *ever* let him make her feel like an inadequate person again. *"Ja."*

They returned to the kitchen, and both women took a seat at the table. Naomi said, "It's settled. Greta will go."

Afraid her sisters would read the fear in her eyes Greta kept her gaze on her hands clasped together on the table. "I'll take the bus there and accompany him in the van on his journey. I'll write to Morris and his bishop and tell them to expect me in four days. That should give them enough time to arrange everything."

"*Gott* willing, you will be home two days later," Naomi added.

Greta let out a deep sigh and looked around the table. "I really don't want to bring him into this house."

The sisters exchanged glances. Clara said, "We feel the same, but perhaps this is a test of our compassion. It is the Christmas season, after all. How can we abandon *Onkel* Morris, ill and alone, knowing that God sent His only Son into this world to teach us to care for one another, even those who hate us?"

"The right thing to do is not always the easy thing to do," Betsy added in resignation.

"Perhaps his illness has shown Morris the error of his ways, and he is ready to mend our family fences," Lizzie suggested in a falsely bright tone.

Greta wouldn't count on it. Of all the ways she had imagined spending her first Christmas at her new home, none of them included sharing it with mean old Morris.

"Joseph, you have very wise granddaughters," Naomi said with a tender smile.

He nodded. "That may be true, but I'm with Greta. I'll take him in, but I don't want the man here, either. Morris will find a way to ruin our Christmas. You mark my words."

Chapter Two

They were going home at last.

Toby Yoder knelt in front of his ten-year-old sister's wheelchair inside the huge lobby of the Fort Wayne Medical Center. The soaring two-story tall glass windows let the light pour in around her. It reflected off the gleaming marble floors and the chrome legs of the chairs and tables near them. Swags of greenery and red bows adorned the front of the large curved cherrywood reception desk while a massive white Christmas tree with blue ornaments and a gleaming silver star dominated the center of the lobby. Every table had a potted poinsettia or an arrangement of cinnamon-scented pinecones in the center.

Signs of the holy season were everywhere, but they couldn't lighten his heart.

Marianne wouldn't look at the sunshine, or the Christmas decorations—or at him. She sat slumped into the corner of the chair as if hiding from the world in a donated black coat that was too big for her. She looked worn to the bone already and she had been up less than half an hour. She was still so weak. His funny, fun-loving and energetic little sister was a shell of her former self and it was his fault.

If it took the rest of his life, he would make it up to her.

He forced a smile for her benefit. "We don't have to leave town today, Marianne. My old roommates won't mind if you want to stay at their apartment. It's not far from here. You can rest up for a few days before we travel to Pennsylvania. I'll make arrangements for another driver to take us then."

She shook her head slightly. "*Nee*. Take me home now," she whispered.

She hadn't spoken more than a few whispered words to him since the fire that took the lives of their parents and put her in the hospital. In spite of that, she managed to make it clear she wanted to go back to Pennsylvania. She didn't want to stay in Indiana.

A non-Amish family walked in through the hospital doors. Several of the children stared openly at Toby and Marianne. Dressed in traditional Amish clothing and wearing a black flat-topped felt hat, Toby knew he stood out from ordinary visitors to the hospital. Although there were large Amish settlements in the area, Amish folks rarely ventured into the heart of the city.

Marianne pulled her oversize black bonnet forward to cover the still raw-looking burns on the left side of her face and neck. She hated people staring at her. A stab of pity took the smile from Toby's face. He would give anything to undo the decisions that had led to her pain, but that wasn't possible. God should have put him in her place that night. She should have been the one left unscathed.

The elevator door across the lobby opened and a nurse came out pushing another wheelchair. In it sat an Amish elder wearing a heavy frown. His pale face was almost as gray as his long beard. A young man in scrubs followed them, pushing a cart laden with several suitcases. He left the cart parked near the door and joined the nurse. "Take care of yourself, Mr. Barkman. Merry Christmas." With a nod, a wink and a thumbs-up to the nurse, he went back to the elevators.

"I don't see why you're kicking me out in the cold. What kind of hospital is this?" Mr. Barkman grumbled.

"We aren't kicking you out, Mr. Barkman. Your driver is on his way. He has picked up your niece at the bus station, and they'll be here soon. You're going home with her."

"That's no comfort to me. My nieces are the cause of this, you know. Their disgraceful behavior shamed me and put all the work of the farm on my shoulders. It was too much for a man my age. You think I'll be better off living with them? Ha! You might as well call the undertaker and be done with it."

"That's no way to talk. Remember what your doctor told you. A positive attitude will help more than any medication." She parked his chair by a sofa in the waiting area.

"That doctor would sing a different tune if he'd had a heart attack and heart surgery. Where are my pain pills?"

"You will need to pick them up at the pharmacy. I have all the instructions on what you need to take and when. I will go over it with you and your niece. You have your nitroglycerin, don't you?"

He nodded and patted his vest pocket. "Pills, pills and more pills. What good have they done me? I'm still a sick man."

She said, "I see a van coming up the drive. I think they're here."

The relief in the nurse's voice brought back Toby's grin. He leaned close to his sister. "You are a much better patient." He hoped for a smile, but he was disappointed. She kept her head lowered.

A long white van pulled to a stop outside the doors. The driver, a portly man in his midforties with curly salt-and-pepper hair hopped out and came around to open the sliding door on the passenger's side. A young Amish woman got out.

"Is that your niece, Mr. Barkman?" the nurse asked.

"That's Greta. The ungrateful hussy. I'm amazed she has the courage to show her face to me."

The nurse rolled her eyes and muttered, "So am I."

Toby happened to catch her glance. She smothered a sheepish grin. It was clear she thought Mr. Barkman's niece would have her hands full.

The outside door opened. The van driver and the woman came inside along with a gust of cold wind. Mr. Barkman's niece stopped a few feet away from her uncle. The driver came straight to Toby.

"Are you Tobias Yoder?" he asked in a booming voice.

Toby rose and held out his hand. "You must be Arles Hooper. Thank you for agreeing to take us to Bird-in-Hand, Pennsylvania. I know it's a very long drive. This is Marianne."

"Pleased to meet you both. I've got several more Amish folks riding with us. It's fortunate for me that so many Amish like to travel this time of year. I've got a full load. I had to make the trip worth my while, you know, with the price of gas and oil. Course you folks don't have to worry about that, what with driving buggies. We won't make it to Bird-in-Hand tonight, but I'll get you there as soon as I can. There's talk of a big winter storm moving this way. I'm hoping to beat it, but I know a few nice, inexpensive motels where we can hunker down if need be."

"That's fine." Toby nodded, but he didn't have the funds for an extended stay at a motel. What little extra he had would be needed when he got to Pennsylvania.

"Good. I have a family named Coblentz with me. There are eight of them, but they are only going as far as Ohio City. I know that's a little bit out of your way, but not much, less than an hour. I'll be taking Mr. Barkman and his niece all the way to Hope Springs, Ohio. From there, it will just be you two. I hope you don't mind the additional passengers."

"We'll be glad of the extra company on the trip, won't we, Marianne?" He spoke to his sister, but his gaze was drawn to Mr. Barkman's niece.

Ungrateful Greta didn't look like a hussy. She wasn't strikingly pretty, but she was pleasant looking. Demurely dressed in a dark blue overcoat and a large black bonnet, she was slightly taller than average. She carried a blue cloth bag over one arm. What little he could see of her hair was a light honey brown. He couldn't be sure from here, but he thought her eyes were light brown, as well.

She stood with her head held high. There was something almost defiant in her stance. Something else he'd noticed…there hadn't been any display of affection or even a greeting between her and her uncle.

Arles left Toby's side and approached Mr. Barkman. "Good to have you with us, sir. I'll do my best to make it an easy journey. Shall I put your things in the van?"

"Greta can do it. She's good with simple tasks," Mr. Barkman snapped.

Toby caught a glimpse of the covert glance she shot her uncle. Her eyes filled with dislike before she looked down and schooled her features into blankness. Toby's interest sharpened. The tension between the uncle and niece was palpable. It might prove to be an uncomfortable trip with these two in the van.

The nurse said, "Please take the bags out, Mr. Hooper. I need to speak with Miss Barkman about her uncle's care."

Toby continued to study the young Amish woman who looked to be in her early twenties. Her knuckles stood out white against her dark clothing where her hands were clenched tightly into fists. She seemed taut as a bowstring.

She glanced his way, and her eyes softened when she caught sight of his sister. A gentle smile curved her lips and changed her features from pleasant looking to sweetly appealing. He found himself smiling in turn. She looked up from his sister and met his gaze.

Appealing was right. Instantly, he felt a strange connection. Her eyes widened. He was right. They were a light, lively golden brown. He couldn't seem to break the contact. Who was Greta Barkman? What was she thinking? He wanted to know.

She looked away first, and his unexpected connection with her was broken. The nurse had called her Miss Barkman, so she wasn't married.

He gave a small shake of his head. Interest in a pretty woman should be the last thing on his mind. He needed to get Marianne home to Pennsylvania, find a job and look after her. She was his priority now. He planned to spend the rest of his life taking care of her. He owed her that much and more.

He laid a comforting hand on her shoulder. She flinched, then grabbed his hand. "You won't leave me, will you?"

The treatment for her burns had been painful, leaving her leery of physical contact, but she didn't want him out of her sight. He knelt in front of her. "Of course not. We're going home to Pennsylvania together."

"I don't want these other people around."

"I know, honey, but it can't be helped. Don't worry. I'll be with you every step of the way."

Greta caught the interplay between the young girl in the wheelchair and the handsome man with her. It was comforting to see such a close relationship. Her own troubled history gave her a heightened sense of awareness about others, particularly young women. The man was a nice-looking Amish fellow with dark hair, intelligent dark eyes and a winning smile. There was something compelling in his gaze that intrigued her.

"There are some things we need to go over, Miss Barkman. It should only take a few minutes," the nurse said, drawing Greta's attention once more.

"Of course." She managed a stiff smile.

"Please ask if you have any questions. I've included my cell phone number at the top of the paperwork. When I spoke with Mr. Hooper about this trip, he assured me you would be able to use his phone if you need to. Mr. Hooper understands that he'll have to make frequent stops for Mr. Barkman's well-being."

"A lot of good that will do. What if I need to lie down?" Morris asked.

"I'll do everything in my power to make you comfortable, *Onkel,*" Greta assured him.

"You and your sisters have brought me nothing but shame and hardship. Traveling with you will not bring me comfort."

Greta pressed her lips together to hold back her comment. She had come prepared to treat her uncle with civility, but his attitude was making it difficult. He hadn't changed at all. If anything, he was openly hostile now. Before, he had taken pains to keep his cruelty hidden.

The nurse pushed Morris toward a nearby door. "We will have more privacy inside our Quiet Room. I'm Mrs. Collins, the discharge nurse for our Cardiac Care Unit."

Greta rushed to hold open the door for them. The nurse said, "Why don't you have a seat, Miss Barkman. I need to review Mr. Barkman's going-home instructions with you both."

She pulled a clipboard from a pocket on the back of the wheelchair and stepped around to face Morris. She held out the clipboard and a pen. "I need your permission to share your medical information with your niece. Would you sign on the bottom, please?"

"I don't see why she needs to know anything."

"Your medications are complex and should you develop

any problems, your niece must know what to do. A patient can't very well take nitroglycerin if they are unconscious. This is hypothetical, of course, but you do see my point, don't you?"

Morris pulled the document toward him and scribbled his name across the bottom. "Tell her anything you like, but I don't have to stay and listen to it."

"Very well. You may wait outside until Mr. Hooper can take you to the van."

Mrs. Collins wheeled Morris out and after a few minutes, the woman returned alone. She smiled as she sat down across from Greta. "I'm sorry. Your uncle has not been the most cooperative patient."

"That doesn't surprise me. Please tell me what I need to know."

The nurse's face softened. "Your uncle sustained a massive heart attack. The doctors here did a triple bypass surgery, but even with restored blood flow, some of his heart muscle has been severely damaged."

"I'm surprised he agreed to the surgery. It is not our way."

"We were surprised, as well, but I'm afraid in spite of the surgery his prognosis is not good."

Greta frowned. "I don't understand."

"He continues to have episodes of chest pain, what we call unstable angina. He has medicine that he needs to take as soon as these episodes begin. The pain is caused by a lack of blood flow to his already weakened heart. Your uncle's heart was so damaged that he is not a candidate for another procedure. The best we can offer is palliative care."

"What does this mean, *palliative?*" Greta thought she understood the sympathy in the woman's words but she needed to be sure.

"It means we want to make your uncle's last months as comfortable as possible. He is not going to get better."

"Morris is dying?" Greta felt the air rush out of her lungs.

Chapter Three

The man who made her life miserable for years would die soon.

Greta took a deep, unsteady breath and looked at the nurse. "Does my uncle know he won't get better?"

Mrs. Collins nodded. "He is aware of his prognosis, but I don't believe that he has accepted it. I'm sorry to give you such bad news. He tells us he has no close family or friends. Frankly, we were all very surprised by that. The Amish people we have treated in the past have been surrounded by caring family and church members."

Greta waited to feel something, anything, but all she felt was numb. Over the years, after some of her worst beatings at his hands, she had prayed that God would call him to judgment. God hadn't answered her then. Why now?

Her common sense reasserted itself. Her uncle's illness was part of God's larger plan. It had nothing to do with the wishes of the scared and angry girl she had once been.

The scared, angry woman she still was.

How many times had she offered her forgiveness up to God? And how many times had her anger raised its ugly head the way it was doing now? She didn't want to hate him. She only wanted to be free of him. And soon she would be.

This news changed so much. She wasn't sure what to

say to him or how to act. It suddenly struck her that this could be his last Christmas.

Greta gripped her bag tightly. "How long do you think he has?"

"Our best guess is a few months. With good care, it could be longer. We can't say for sure."

"Of course. Only God knows when our time here is done. Is he…is he suffering?"

"Angina attacks can be painful and very frightening, but on the whole he isn't in pain. He does tire easily so make sure he gets enough rest."

"I will." Greta looked at the floor. Could she take care of him? Why was God placing the burden on her?

The nurse handed Greta several pamphlets and a type-written list. "These are some important points for you to know. They cover diet suggestions, exercise, pain management, things that can make his quality of life better. I also have some information on end-of-life issues. You may want to look over this and discuss it with your family members and perhaps your minister. And with Mr. Barkman when he is ready."

Greta took the pamphlets and tucked them into her bag. "You mentioned something about medicines?"

"Yes. These are his prescriptions. I will give your driver directions to a pharmacy near here. Your uncle has a vial of small white pills with him called nitroglycerin. He is to put one under his tongue at the first sign of chest pain. I have written out what you need to do if that doesn't help. I know this is a lot for you to take in. Are you sure you are okay with this?"

"I believe I understand everything you have said. What about his bill?"

"That's been covered in full."

By his church no doubt. At least his congregation had done that for him even if they wouldn't take him in. It was strange that her uncle's bishop hadn't mentioned the fact in his letter.

Mrs. Collins handed over a business card. "This is my personal number. Call me anytime you have questions. Day or night, it doesn't matter. I only wish we could have done more for your uncle."

"He is in God's hands. It is as the Lord wills."

"Yes. We are all in God's hands. We all struggle to do the best we can in an imperfect world. I pray God gives both you and your uncle the comfort you need."

She rose to her feet and left Greta alone.

Toby spoke to the driver who was pushing the empty cart inside after having loaded Mr. Barkman's things. "Arles, is it all right if we get settled in the van?"

"Sure. Do you need a hand?"

"*Nee,* I can manage."

Mr. Barkman was slowly wheeling himself toward the door. There was no sign of his niece yet.

Arles caught sight of him. "Just a minute, sir, and I'll help you."

Mr. Barkman grunted but didn't answer.

Toby pulled on his coat. From a nearby chair, he picked up the duffel bag that contained all his and his sister's worldly belongings. The fire hadn't left them much. Neighbors and his coworkers had contributed clothing and essentials. He had enough money to pay their way and get by on this trip, but not much else. He figured they could wait until they were back in Pennsylvania and he was working again to purchase anything else they might need. When he could find work.

His mother's sister and her husband were taking them in. With eleven children of her own, his aunt assured him that two more would hardly be noticed. He was grateful for her kindness. She believed living with a big and lively family would help Marianne recover. He prayed she was right.

He pushed his sister's wheelchair out the sliding glass doors and up to the van. He held out his hand to steady her as she gingerly stood. She wavered slightly but managed to step into the van. He worried that she was still so weak. She should have been gaining strength, but she wasn't. It was as if she didn't want to get better.

Inside the van were three rows of double seats along the left side and a row of three single seats along the right side upholstered in brown and cream vinyl. A narrow aisle led to a full bench seat at the rear. There was a luggage compartment behind that.

The passenger's seat by the driver, the first two rows and all the single seats were taken by the Coblentz family, a tall, thin father, a plump mother with four stair-step blond boys and an older woman with a toddler beside her. Toby nodded to the occupants as he followed Marianne. She bypassed the last empty row and went straight to the bench in the back. Toby propped his duffel bag in the corner and sat down beside her. She lay down on the bench.

He took off his coat and folded it into a pillow for her. "Here. Use this."

She took it from him without a word.

Leaning back, he closed his eyes as exhaustion took over. He was eager to get to Bird-in-Hand where his aunt had a real bed waiting for him. He'd spent most of the past two months sleeping in a chair or on the couch in the burn-unit waiting room and then on a cot in his sister's room. He hadn't left her side for more than an hour since she had been transferred out of the ICU. She quickly became panicked when he was out of sight.

After a little while, the outside door of the van opened again. Toby watched as Mr. Barkman was helped in by the driver. He sat down and sighed heavily as he put his cane on the seat beside him. A few minutes later, Greta got in. She stopped beside her uncle, waiting for him to move his cane so she could sit down.

He glared at her. "I may have to travel in the same van but I refuse to sit beside this sinner. She and her sisters have been shunned by our church. She is under the *Bann*."

Everyone in the van turned to look at her in shock. Then, one by one, the adults turned away from her, their backs rigid with disapproval. Toby wondered what she had done to earn such condemnation from her congregation.

She looked around. No one else made room for her. She had no choice but to move to the back where he sat.

She kept her gaze lowered, but her cheeks were blazing red with embarrassment. "Sir, may I sit here?"

Chapter Four

Greta waited for the man in the backseat to answer her. Humiliation burned deep in her chest. Her hopes that Morris had seen the error of his ways and had become a reformed man were nothing more than wishes in the wind. He hadn't changed. And now she was taking him to the one place where she and her sisters had been safe from his venom.

The young girl lying on the bench seat started to sit up, but the man stopped her. He moved his duffel bag from beside him to the floor. "Please, have a seat."

"Danki." Greta maneuvered past his long legs. She sat beside him and pressed herself into the corner wishing she could sink through the seat and onto the pavement outside. She couldn't imagine what the other passengers must be thinking.

Baptized members of their faith were forbidden to have close contact with a shunned member. That this young man offered her a place beside him meant that he had not yet taken his vows. She crossed her arms tightly over her bag and made herself as small as possible. She should have spoken up. She should have refuted her uncle's claim, but years of remaining silent while Morris chastised her in front of others had fastened her tongue to the top of her mouth.

They wouldn't believe her, anyway. They would believe him. He was a man and an elder.

"Are you all right?" the young man beside her asked quietly.

She glanced his way and saw honest compassion in his expression. His small gesture of kindness brought tears to Greta's eyes. She nodded, too upset to speak.

She should have expected her uncle's rebuff, but after living with her loving grandfather in a happy home for the past eight months she had forgotten how easily her uncle could make her feel like dirt. All it took was a few distasteful words in his condescending voice to make her feel like an unwanted child again. She hadn't come nearly as far as she thought she had. If only she could be strong like Lizzie.

The driver got in. "Are we ready?"

A general murmur of consent was enough for him. "Okeydokey. I've been told that Mr. Barkman can't ride more than an hour without stopping. We will stop for lunch at a little place I know in Van Wert about an hour from now. Then, I'll drop the Coblentz family just south of there in Ohio City and we'll get back on the road to Hope Springs, Ohio. That's my plan. Mr. Barkman, are you doing okay?"

"No one cares so let's get going."

The driver turned in his seat. "Sir, if you're not feeling well we should inform the hospital staff right away."

"I'm good enough. I'd rather die on the road than go back inside this poor excuse for a hospital. Drive on."

Arles shrugged. "All right. Mr. Yoder, is your sister doing okay?"

"She is, *danki*."

"Good. We have one stop at the pharmacy to make and then we'll be on the road."

They left the hospital behind, and Mr. Hooper maneuvered the van skillfully through the city traffic. He stopped at the pharmacy the nurse had suggested. Greta had to pass by everyone to get out of the van. She was aware of the covert looks cast her way but decided to ignore them. It was useless to protest now.

After she returned with her uncle's pills, Mr. Hooper soon had them out on the highway heading east. A few minutes later Greta's seatmate asked, "Do you have enough room?"

"Am I crowding you?" She scooted away from him another inch. She had been so wrapped up in her humiliation that she had failed to pay attention to her surroundings.

She glanced at the girl beside him. "Is your sister comfortable?"

"I think she's asleep."

"Has she been sick long?"

"She was injured in a house fire two months ago. She suffered smoke inhalation and burns to her head and neck."

"How terrible."

"Her lungs were damaged by the smoke. She was on the ventilator for several weeks which is why her voice is so weak. God in His mercy saw fit to save her, and I'm grateful. I don't know what I would do without her."

She heard the sadness in his voice. "A fire is such a terrible thing. Was anyone else in your family hurt?"

"My parents perished."

"Oh, I'm very sorry."

"Has your uncle been ill long?"

Greta looked out the window. "A few weeks. He had a heart attack. I will tell you because I know you are wondering and you have been kind. My sisters and I left our uncle's church here in Indiana under difficult circumstances. If the church placed us in the *Bann,* this is the first I have heard about it. We have been accepted into an Old Order congregation in Hope Springs, Ohio, where we live with our grandfather. I am a member of good standing in that community although I have not yet taken my vows."

Morris had been listening. He turned in his seat. "Does

your bishop know he harbors such an unchristian family of snakes to his bosom? Does he know your grandfather set his dog on me? I still have the scars. I will make it clear you are not fit to be members when I meet your bishop."

Greta wanted to vanish. She wanted to crawl inside herself. She wasn't brave the way Lizzie was brave. What would Lizzie do? She would stand up to him. She wouldn't accept this humiliation.

No, she wouldn't.

Greta raised her chin. She wasn't bold, but she knew what Lizzie would say. "Bishop Zook knows our story well, *Onkel.* I think you are the one he will be keeping an eye on. But why are we talking about unchristian behavior? Forgiveness is God's command to us."

Morris muttered something again, but Greta couldn't hear what it was. He turned his back on her. She clamped her lower lip between her teeth to keep it from trembling. She had spoken back to him for the first time in her life.

It was empowering to speak her mind. She didn't have to be bullied by him on this trip. No one here knew her or cared how she behaved. So what if they thought she was disrespectful. They didn't know the truth.

Greta glanced at Toby and found him watching her closely. She quickly looked down. She was not behaving as a humble maiden should. He must think her very brazen.

"Did your grandfather really sic the dog on your uncle?" The raspy whisper came from Toby's sister as she sat up. She held her bonnet pulled forward to cover the left side of her face.

Greta shook her head and whispered back, "No one set the dog on him. *Onkel* Morris doesn't like dogs and our dog, Duncan, didn't like him. Duncan thought he was protecting us."

Marianne said, "Animals know if people are nice or not."

Greta smiled. The child was so right. Leaning forward, Greta winked at her. "I agree. Duncan is an excellent judge of character."

Toby watched in amazement as his sister smiled at their seatmate and giggled. It was a tiny gurgle more than a giggle, but it was the most emotion he'd seen from her since the fire.

A great weight lifted off his chest. Until this moment, he hadn't been aware of the pressure. The glimpse of the girl she used to be filled his heart with joy.

Had leaving the hospital triggered this improvement, or was it the infectious smile of their new traveling companion? Perhaps it was a combination of the two. Either way, he was relieved to see this small sign of progress.

"My name is Greta Barkman," she told his sister.

"I'm Marianne."

"And I'm Toby Yoder," he added.

"It's nice to meet you both. Do you have a dog, Marianne?" Greta asked.

His sister shook her head. Toby read the regret in the turned-down corners of her mouth. He said, "We may have to look into getting one."

Marianne's eyes brightened, but then she shook her head and leaned away from him.

He said, "I know we won't be able to keep a dog at our aunt's house. She doesn't like dogs, but we'll have our own home again someday. When we do, we will get a dog. I promise."

She sighed deeply but didn't say anything else. Greta sat back and turned to look out the window. It seemed her friendliness was reserved for his sister. After a few minutes, she opened her bag and pulled out a wooden hoop with a length of white fabric secured in it. Half the circle was filled with blue cross-stitched flowers. Deftly, she began creating another row.

He tried to focus on the passing scenery. It wasn't often he had the chance to ride in a car. It was amazing how quickly the farms and fields slipped behind them. Empty fields waiting for spring to bring back the green. Red barns and occasional blue road signs were the only bright colors besides the blue sky. Toby soon grew bored with the winter landscape and began watching Greta again.

She had her circle completed in no time. Loosening the hoop, she withdrew her fabric and replaced it with a fresh square from her bag. Marianne shifted on her seat, and he glanced her way. She was leaning forward to watch Greta work, too. It wasn't long before Greta noticed.

"Do you cross-stitch?"

Toby touched his chest. "Me? Sure."

A smile played at the corner of her mouth. "It's an unusual pastime for a man."

"I would call it a learning experience. I remember my first as if it were yesterday."

She arched an eyebrow. "Really?"

"He's doesn't know how," Marianne whispered.

"That's what you think, little sister. Grandmother taught me to do it when I was your age."

He could see Marianne didn't believe him. He had trouble keeping a straight face. "It's true. She made me sit in the corner and fill her hoop with one phrase over and over again. Her hoop was much bigger than yours, Greta."

"And what was that phrase?" Greta asked.

"*I will not tell a lie. I will not tell a lie. I will not tell a lie.* It took me four hours to finish it to her satisfaction. The lesson stuck."

Greta chuckled. "I think I would like to meet your grandmother."

"She lives with her widowed sister near Bird-in-Hand. You can ask her about the story. She'll tell you it's true."

"I don't doubt you, but I was actually asking Marianne if she knew how to cross-stitch?"

"Do you?" He looked at his sister.

She shook her head.

"I'm sure Greta can show you how it's done."

"I'd be delighted. It's easy. These are panels that will go down the center of a quilt my sisters and I are stitching."

"Switch places with me." He rose and let his sister slide across the seat to sit beside Greta. She was soon engrossed in Greta's instructions, leaving him free to watch both of them.

Within a few minutes, Marianne had the hoop and the needle and thread on her lap. "What if I make a mistake? I don't want to ruin it."

"We all make mistakes. It would be a shame not to learn something new because you're afraid you won't get it right. Besides, you will not ruin it. I can easily undo the stitches."

Marianne's efforts were tentative at first, but under Greta's gentle guidance, she soon grew more confident. She was actually talking, even if her voice was still a hoarse whisper. Toby was surprised when the driver turned off the highway into the parking lot of a small diner. Were they in Van Wert already? An hour had gone by very quickly.

Arles turned to address his passengers. "I'd like everyone to be back in the van in thirty minutes. That should give us all plenty of time to eat and walk about a little. Mr. Barkman, how are you doing?"

"Well enough. I don't imagine the food will be good at a place like this."

"It's got to be better than the hospital food," Toby said as he slipped into his coat.

The driver got out and came around to open the door.

The Coblentz family piled out quickly. Morris stayed where he was so Toby got out next and held out his hand for his sister. She took it and stepped carefully onto the pavement. He was worried that this outing would be too much for her, but she seemed to be doing okay.

He moved back to let Greta out. She was about to step down when her uncle rose. His cane slid to the side between her feet. Greta tripped and fell headlong out of the van. Toby lunged to catch her.

Chapter Five

Finding herself in Toby's arms took Greta's breath away. Strong and rock steady, he held her as if she weighed nothing at all. She gripped his shoulders to get her feet under her. The feel of his firm muscles beneath her fingers sent a rush of excitement through her veins. It tightened her chest and made it hard to breathe. She licked her suddenly dry lips as she looked up at him.

Electricity seemed to shimmer between them like the glow of distant lightning. His dark brown eyes widened in surprise. Did he feel it, too? She couldn't tear her gaze away from his expressive face.

"Are you all right?" Marianne asked.

The child's whispery voice brought Greta back to the present. What was wrong with her? No man had ever had this effect on her.

She slowly withdrew from Toby's embrace. His cheeks blossomed with a dull red color. Was it her imagination, or was he reluctant to let her go?

He spoke to Morris. "You must be more careful."

Morris pushed out of his seat. "It was an accident. What you want me to say?"

After stepping down from the van, he looked at the people who stood staring at him. He straightened and his frown deepened. "I said it was an accident."

"I'm fine, *Onkel.* Do not you worry yourself about it," Greta said quietly.

"He should say he's sorry," Marianne muttered.

"And your parents should teach you not to disrespect your elders," Morris grumbled.

Tears welled up in Marianne's eyes, and she pressed her face against Toby's side.

"Why she crying? What did I say?" Morris demanded. Everyone was still clustered around the side of the van.

Toby's face reflected his deep pain as he gazed at his sister. "Our parents were killed in a fire a few months ago."

"I'm sorry to hear that. How was I to know? My doctor said I have to walk." Morris shouldered his way through the onlookers and began walking along the sidewalk in front of the restaurant.

"I should go with him in case he has trouble," Greta said.

"Do you want me to stay with you?" Toby offered.

She shook her head. "I'm sure Marianne would like a soda or a cup of tea."

"All right. Can I order anything for you?"

"I would dearly love a cup of coffee."

Greta took a seat on the bench out front where she could keep an eye on Morris. It was growing colder. A bank of gray clouds shut out the sun in the west. She buttoned the top buttons of her coat and pulled on her gloves. She was surprised when Marianne sat down beside her.

"Don't you want to go inside?" Greta asked.

"*Nee,* people stare at me." Her voice was weaker than before. Greta could see how tired she was.

"In that case, please join me. I'm not really hungry, but I may have some dessert when my uncle is finished with his walk."

She looked around for Toby and saw him waiting beside the door with his hands shoved in his coat pockets.

She motioned toward the diner with her head. He nodded his understanding. She would watch over Marianne while he went in.

"What sorts of desserts do you like, Marianne?"

"Ice cream and pie. I hear a kitten. There it is." Marianne pointed toward Morris.

A small calico cat was rubbing against his leg. He nudged it away with his cane, but the cat came back, stood on its hind legs and pawed at his trousers. It began meowing loudly.

"Your uncle must like cats."

"As far as I know, he doesn't care for any living thing except himself."

Greta bit her lip as she realized she shouldn't have spoken like that in front of the child. She shouldn't even have such thoughts. Her feelings about her uncle were hard to hide, but he was ill. He deserved some kindness although she wasn't sure she had any to offer.

Morris pushed the cat away and walked on. Greta glanced at Marianne. "I like ice cream, too. Chocolate is my favorite. But when it's cold outside like this I like pumpkin pie with whipped topping."

Marianne pulled away and wrinkled her nose.

Greta laughed. Cupping her fingers under her chin, she tapped her cheek with one finger in mock concentration. "I think you are someone who likes coconut pie."

Shaking her head, Marianne stuck out her tongue.

"Strawberry rhubarb?" Greta glanced toward her uncle, keeping one eye on him while she engaged Marianne in conversation. He bent to scratch the cat's head.

"Peach," Marianne stated in a harsh whisper. Greta wasn't sure if it was the cold or fatigue, but the girl's voice was definitely weaker. She needed to rest it.

Just then, Toby returned bearing gifts. He held three foam cups in his hands. He set them on the end of the bench and passed them around. "Coffee for you, Greta, and hot chocolate for you, Marianne."

"Danki." Greta took the beverage from him.

Marianne eagerly accepted hers. He sat down and took a sip from his cup. "Not bad."

"Delicious," Greta added. She glanced toward Morris. He was bent over. Was he talking to the cat? The animal paced back and forth in front of him still meowing.

Greta looked down at the drink in her hands as she tried to quell the bitterness that rose in her throat. He could treat a stray cat with kindness but not his own kin.

She focused on Toby. "Your sister was telling me that she likes peach pie. I have a friend whose husband loves peach pie. His name is Levi Beachy and he makes buggies in our town. What do you do, Toby?"

"I work at a factory that builds RVs in Fort Wayne, or I did until recently. Before that, our family lived in Pennsylvania. There, I was a wood-carver, but the shop where my father and I were employed closed and we couldn't find work. That's why we moved to Fort Wayne. I'm not sure what I will do now, but Marianne and I will figure that out together."

He looked at his sister as she sipped her chocolate with relish, and he smiled softly. Toby was a kind and caring brother. It made Greta miss her sisters. She would love to have them here with her now.

The cat jumped in her lap scaring the wits out of her. She jerked in fright, sloshing hot coffee on her hand. The cat ran back to her uncle. Greta saw him leaning heavily on his cane and clutching his chest.

Greta dropped her drink and hurried toward him.

"Are you all right, *Onkel?*" she asked when she reached his side.

"Need my...pills." He was fumbling at his vest pocket.

Greta quickly extracted a small vial. Her fingers trembled as she opened the lid and shook a pill into his hand. He put it under his tongue.

Toby slipped his arms around the old man's shoulders and behind his knees. He lifted him like a child, carried him to the bench and laid him down. Morris was breathing heavily. Toby looked at Greta. "Should we call an ambulance?"

"Ja."

"Nee." Morris shook his head. "It's better."

"Are you sure?" She knelt in front of him.

He gave her a sour look. "You won't have to pay for my burial yet, Mouse."

Greta took a deep breath and disguised her shame with a show of indifference. It was a skill she had learned well living with him. But Lizzie wouldn't let such a jab go unanswered. Greta narrowed her eyes. "That's good to know, *Onkel.* My expense account is woefully inadequate at the moment."

That took him aback. It did her good to see his surprise. The mouse hadn't roared, but it squeaked.

Was there any way to reach him? To make him see how hurtful his words could be? Had he really tried to make her fall out of the van, or was it an accident as he claimed? She couldn't be sure.

When she and her sisters had lived with him, his abuse had been overt. A beating with a belt or with a wooden rod. That punishment wasn't available to him with so many people around. She didn't want to believe the worst of him, but she had never seen anything else.

"Help me up," he said, reaching for her hand.

She hesitated. Why should she? Why had she even come?

A second later, she knew the answer as clearly as if God had spoken to her. She was here because it was the right thing to do. Returning evil for evil did no one any good. Taking his hand, she pulled him into a sitting position.

He sighed heavily. "I would like a cup of tea."

She kept one hand under his elbow as he stood. Toby stayed close until she had Morris seated at a booth inside the diner. Toby and Marianne chose their own table and sat away from the group. Marianne sat next to the wall, sinking into the corner as if hiding from the world. Greta's heart went out to her.

Morris was watching them, too. "Why does she keep her hand at the side of her face all the time? Is she looking for attention?"

"I think she is self-conscious about the scars on her neck and face. She was burned in the house fire that killed her parents."

"They aren't noticeable scars. She's vain."

Compelled to defend the sweet child, Greta glared at her uncle. "To a girl that age they must seem enormous and ghastly. She deserves our kindness not our judgment."

He turned his attention to the waitress and ordered tea. Greta ordered a cup of soup and a slice of peach pie.

Her uncle's color improved steadily. He soon seemed to be his old self. He complained that the tea was lukewarm and sent it back. Then he asked for a glass of ice because it arrived too hot to drink.

When he finished his tea, he rose and headed for the restrooms at the back of the diner. He stumbled and staggered sideways a step before regaining his balance and heading on. Greta caught Toby's eye. He nodded and then indicated his sister with a glance in her direction. Greta nodded, too. Toby rose to follow her uncle while Greta moved to sit with Marianne. It was amazing how easily they communicated with only a shared look. He wasn't like anyone she had met before. She quickly pushed her interest in him to the back of her mind.

Taking her uneaten pie as a pretense, she sat down at the same table with the child. "Would you like my pie? I don't have room for it."

Marianne nodded. Greta pushed the dish toward her. She folded her hands and smiled. "I have always wanted to travel to Pennsylvania. Is it pretty?"

Marianne nodded again.

"Are you and your brother visiting family there?"

"We're going to live with my *aenti*."

"You and your brother?"

"Ja."

"I'm very sorry about your parents. My parents have gone to heaven, too, so I know your sadness. I miss them although I know they are happy with God. I'm not alone, though. I have three sisters and we all look out for each other the way your brother has been looking out for you on this trip. You are blessed that he was spared."

Marianne didn't say anything, so Greta forged ahead. "It's hard to talk about the people we have lost, but you don't have to be afraid. You can tell me about it."

"Nee, you will hate me."

"We must never hate anyone, Marianne." If only she could follow her own advice.

"It was my fault they died." Marianne pushed the rest of the uneaten pie aside and got up from the table. She rushed outside leaving Greta to wonder exactly what had happened to the child's family.

After paying her bill, Greta went outside, too. The Coblentz family was already in the van. Greta got in and sat at the back with Marianne. The girl lay curled onto her side facing the back of the seat. Greta couldn't see her face. "I'm sorry if I upset you."

The child ignored her. Greta chewed her lower lip. She had been trying to help but she may have made things worse. Morris and Toby came out of the restaurant a short time later. Mr. Hooper started the van as Toby climbed in behind Morris. A loud thunk from the engine and a cat's screech startled everyone.

Arles and Toby went to the front of the vehicle. Greta got out, and Marianne followed her.

Chapter Six

Arles lifted the hood of the van. Toby leaned in and pulled the limp cat free. It was the same calico that had fawned over Greta's uncle earlier. The poor thing had been hit by the fan blade. It bore an awful gash on the side of its neck and most of its left ear was missing.

"Help her," Marianne pleaded with tears in her eyes.

Greta quickly offered her handkerchief. "Use this to stop the bleeding."

"Danki." Toby pressed the cloth to the animal's head.

"We must find the owner. The poor thing needs a veterinarian," Greta said.

Toby looked around. "Maybe the restaurant owner or one of the customers will know who she belongs to. I'll go ask."

"I'll take her," Greta offered. She unbuttoned her coat. Toby handed the animal to her. She wrapped the poor thing in her long apron and tried to soothe her.

The cat started crying pitifully. Marianne watched with wide frightened eyes.

Toby rushed into the restaurant. He caught sight of the cook, a middle-aged *Englisch* fellow with a large stained apron tied around his ample middle. "We need some help. A cat has been injured. Perhaps you can tell us who owns it."

"I doubt it, but let me take a look." He followed Toby

outside and adjusted his glasses to peer at the cat in Greta's arms.

"That's one of Mrs. Alcorn's critters. The old woman died a few months ago. The cats are strays now. Some of the neighbors feed this one, but it won't go inside any of their houses. The old lady had heart trouble. She always said this cat would let her know when she was about to have one of her spells."

"Perhaps that was why she was pawing at my uncle's legs," Greta said. "She sensed he was about to have an attack."

"Animals have remarkable senses," Toby said. "Can you tell us where we can find a veterinarian? This poor animal is suffering."

The cook pointed down a side street. "Doc Harley has a clinic out near the edge of town. You can't miss it."

Arles said, "I can't ask these folks to wait while we take the cat to the vet."

"We can't leave the poor thing lying here in the street." Greta glared at the driver.

"I wasn't suggesting that. This man can take care of it."

The cook shook his head. "I've got a business to run, and I have customers waiting." He turned and strode away.

There was no way Toby was going to leave this animal to fend for itself. He'd just have to hire another driver if Arles wouldn't help. "You can travel on without Marianne and me. I'll get our bag out of the van. We will expect a refund."

Scratching his head, Arles said, "Let's don't be hasty. I reckon we can take a few minutes to turn the cat over to the veterinarian. Okay?"

"That's all we're asking," Toby said.

Everyone got back into the van and Greta, with the cat wrapped in her apron, took her place in the back. Marianne sat beside her. Greta tried to reassure the child. "Don't worry. Someone is going to look after her."

Doc Harley turned out to be a woman in her sixties with short kinky gray hair, a rumpled smock and a no-nonsense manner. She was able to see them after only a brief wait. She examined the cat and smiled at Marianne who was clinging to Greta's side. "I think it looks worse than it is. Cats are very resilient creatures. She will do fine."

"But she doesn't have an ear," Marianne whispered.

"She will look unusual, but she will still be able to hear. This laceration on her neck is going to need a few stitches. Other than that, I think she's in pretty good shape. She could use a little more meat on her bones. Has she been eating normally?"

"According to the man at the restaurant, she's a stray that belonged to Mrs. Alcorn," Toby said.

"Oh, yes, our resident cat lady. I thought this one looked familiar. It's the one she called Christmas. The little stray showed up at her house on Christmas morning a year ago. She was very attached to this one. It's a shame that no one took her after Mrs. Alcorn passed away. If this isn't your cat, are you still willing to pay for her care?"

Toby's funds were limited. He looked at the others. Morris shook his head, "I have no money to spend on a cat."

"If we leave her here, will you take care of her?" Marianne asked.

The vet shook her head. "I'm afraid I don't have room to look after every stray cat that comes this way. I'll turn her over to the county animal shelter. They'll try to find someone to adopt her."

"No one will love her because she's ugly now," Marianne said sadly and reached out to stroke the cat's back.

Toby heard the pain in his sister's voice and knew she

was expressing her own fears. He wanted so much to help her, but he didn't know how.

Greta said, "She's a lovely cat. A missing ear and a few scars won't change that. I'll pay for her care today, and I'll take her home."

"All right." The vet smiled brightly. "Let me take her into surgery to clean these cuts and stitch her up. You can have a seat in the waiting room. It may take an hour or so."

As the vet walked away, Marianne looked up at Greta. "Are you sure you want to keep her? People will stare and make fun of her because she's different."

"You don't intend to drag that cat along with us, do you? Leave it here," Morris said, his voice laced with disgust.

Greta's back straightened. "I do intend to take Christmas with us. She needs a home, and I like her. I don't care that she looks different. She has a good heart and that is more important than her appearance. She tried to help you. We just weren't smart enough to know what she was trying to tell us."

Toby admired the way she stood up to her grumpy uncle and gave his sister a gentle lesson, as well. Looks were not everything. Goodness mattered.

"Foolishness, that's all it is." Morris settled in a waiting room chair. Marianne sat down a few chairs away from him.

Arles rubbed his chin. "I feel responsible for the poor thing, but I have people waiting in the van. What do I tell them?"

Toby slipped his hands in his pockets. "Didn't you say you were taking the Coblentzes's to Ohio City? Can't you drop them off and come back to pick us up?"

"You know, that's a good idea. I'll be back soon as I can." He grinned and headed out the door, clearly relieved to resume his schedule.

Toby took a seat beside Marianne. He picked up a magazine and thumbed through it. He was surprised when she spoke to him. "*Mamm* said I had a good heart."

It wasn't much, but it was a start. His heart expanded with love for his sister. "*Mamm* always spoke the truth. She loved you very much. She loves you even from heaven."

Marianne didn't reply. She got to her feet and went to look through the magazine rack.

He laid his magazine aside and looked at Greta standing by the window. Pushing out of his chair, he went to thank her.

Greta folded her arms and stared out at the gray sky as she waited. Toby came and stood beside her. Quietly, he said, "I appreciate what you're doing for the cat. It means a lot to my sister. I would like to reimburse you for part of this cost. If you would give me your address, I will send you the money when I can."

"Don't worry about the money. I'm just glad that I'm able to help. Unlike some people," she glanced over her shoulder at her uncle.

"Don't be too hard on him. Not everyone believes we have a responsibility to care for all God's creatures."

"But you do." She looked at him and saw only sincerity and kindness in his face. He had a nice face. The planes and angles of it gave him a rugged look, but they softened when he smiled and his smile reached his eyes, making them sparkle.

He said, "I like animals. Dogs, cats, horses, cows."

"Sheep?" she asked.

"I don't know any sheep personally, but I'm sure I would find something to like about them. They look…fluffy."

"Only until they are sheared. Then they look naked and embarrassed." She pressed her hand to her mouth as heat rose in her face. Why had she said that?

He chuckled. "You seem to know your sheep well."

She giggled at her own foolishness. "I live with my grandfather. He raises them. Spend ten minutes with him and his hired man, Carl, and you will learn far more about sheep that you ever thought possible."

"Do sheep get along with cats?" He took a step closer and leaned one shoulder against the wall. His nearness sent a wave of awareness shooting along her nerve endings. She was stunned by a compelling urge to move closer to him, too.

She didn't, but she wanted to. Looking down to hide that longing, she said, "As far as I know. I am a little concerned about our dog, Duncan. He's not a cat lover."

"Maybe he'll make an exception for a cat named Christmas." The sweet, low timbre of his voice sent her pulse racing.

"Perhaps he will." She tried to get a grip on her runaway emotions. He was making polite conversation and nothing more. What was wrong with her? She wasn't the kind of woman to get silly over a man. She was practical and levelheaded. So why did she feel giddy and happy when he was close?

She stole a sidelong glance at him and found him regarding her intently.

What was he thinking? Did he find her attractive?

Foolish thought. She glanced away and saw her uncle watching them with a sour look on his face. Instantly, she was back in his house, hearing his angry voice belittle her attempts to gain his affection. Anger rose up to choke her. Shame burned like acid in her stomach.

Toby said, "I'm grateful that you have been kind to my sister and I wanted to thank you for that. Having you along is making this trip much easier on her."

Greta gripped her hands together. If he knew the kind of person she was underneath the calm face she wore, he wouldn't want his sister having anything to do with her.

* * *

Toby wanted to see Greta smile again. There was something about the gleam in her eyes and the delicate curve of her lips that warmed him and made him smile in return. There hadn't been much happiness in his life in the past two months, but this woman gave him hope. Hope that he and his sister could find their way back to each other. Greta seemed to be the oil that calmed their troubled waters. Marianne responded to her in a way she hadn't responded to the nurses or therapists she had seen in the hospital.

Maybe he was being ridiculous. He'd known Greta for less than two hours, but somehow it felt as if he had known her for a very long time. Tomorrow, they would part company. It saddened him to think he would never see her again.

"What's wrong?" she asked.

She read him too easily. "I was thinking that it's a shame our journey will be over so soon."

A hint of color rose in her cheeks. She focused her gaze out the window. "It has been interesting."

"Much more interesting than I thought it would be."

"What's taking that doctor so long?" Morris asked, shifting in his chair and drawing Toby's attention.

Marianne came to stand in front of him and held out a newspaper. "Would you like something to read?"

"There's nothing else to do." He took it from her.

"Du bishcht wilkumm," she whispered primly and sat in the chair beside him.

Toby shot a quick grin at Greta and kept his voice low. "That's the first time I've heard *you're welcome* sound like a reprimand."

Morris scowled at Marianne but nodded once. *"Danki."*

"At least she got him to say *thank you*. That's more than I have ever done." The chill in Greta's tone smothered Toby's mirth and caused him to look at her closely.

All sign of emotion had vanished from her face. Whatever was wrong between Greta and her uncle, it wasn't as simple as a grumpy elder making travel difficult.

She abruptly headed for the door. "I need some air."

Chapter Seven

Toby started to follow Greta. He wanted to know what was wrong, wanted to help if he could. He opened the door, but Marianne shot out of her chair and rushed to his side, her eyes wide with fright as she clutched his arm. "Where are you going?"

Toby had his own troubles to deal with. He should be concentrating on his sister and not on a woman he'd just met. "No place. I was looking for our van, but Arles isn't back yet."

As he watched Greta walk out to the road, he knew he was kidding himself. He couldn't ignore her even if he tried. Something about her touched him in a way no other woman had.

Tomorrow she will vanish from my life and there's nothing I can do about it. We live hundreds of miles apart. How would I see her? There could be someone special in her life already. This is crazy.

Sighing heavily, he closed the door and led Marianne back to her seat. She hung on to his arm until he sat down, her worried eyes glued to his face. He tried to soothe her. "I know *Aenti* Linda doesn't like dogs, but I wonder if she likes cats?"

Marianne relaxed and smiled slightly. "She had one named Boots…when she and *Mamm* were little."

"Did she? I never knew that."

"*Mamm* told me. Boots was yellow with white paws."

Morris rattled his paper as he turned the page. "They shouldn't be made into pets. God created them to catch vermin."

"*Mamm* said Boots caught lots of mice."

Morris huffed his displeasure and raised the paper to hide behind. Toby wondered if he could pry a little more information about Greta from her uncle. "I heard Arles say you and your niece are going to Hope Springs. Where is that exactly?"

"Between Millersburg and Sugarcreek in Holmes County."

"Greta mentioned she had sisters. How many are there?"

Morris folded his paper and glared at Toby. "I have four ungrateful, spiteful nieces. It's a blessing that my brother is gone. To see his daughters turn their back on their family the way they did would have broken his heart. Greta is a shrew."

Toby was taken aback by the harshness of his words. "I'm sorry to hear that. Greta seems like a nice woman."

"Proverbs 31:30. 'Favour is deceitful, and beauty is vain: but a woman that feareth the Lord, she shall be praised.' I tried to teach her to fear the Lord, but she did not listen. Do not be fooled by her. Do not believe what she says about me."

Toby fell silent, reluctant to listen to anything else Morris had to say, but the old man's words confirmed Toby's earlier feeling. There was more wrong between Greta and her uncle than met the eye.

Marianne tugged on Toby's sleeve. He leaned down to hear her weak whisper, "Greta is nice. I like her."

"I like her, too. You should rest your voice now," he said softly.

She nodded. He sat back and stared at the door, waiting for Greta to return. Everything happened for a reason.

Everything was part of God's plan. He had a purpose in sending the cat to them. There was a reason Toby and his sister had been chosen to share a ride with Greta and her uncle. Perhaps somehow they were meant to help each other. He prayed that was true.

Greta walked along the narrow roadway in front of the animal clinic with her eyes downcast and her hands clenched. She prayed for patience. She prayed for strength. She prayed to hold forgiveness in her heart. It was wrong to stay angry and bitter. She knew that. Her inability to find true forgiveness for her uncle's transgressions made her unworthy to be a member of the Amish faith. One more thing her uncle had taken from her.

No, she couldn't think that way.

If only her sisters were here to counsel her. She needed them now as she had always needed them. Their loving presence in her life was a true gift from God. Without each other, she had no idea how they would have endured life with their uncle.

She stopped and raised her face to the sky. "I thank You for Your mercy, Lord. Please help me. Curb my tongue so I don't say spiteful things to him. Make me remember that he is ill and alone. Let me find the compassion to make his final days comfortable. You alone are the judge of mankind, for only You can see into our hearts. I don't want to harbor this ill will inside me, Lord. Cast it out. Please, cast it out."

Praying eased her agitation and helped her regain a measure of calm. She needed to remember that she was never alone. God was with her, watching her, holding her up as she dealt with every trial in her life, not just her uncle.

Although her faith in God had wavered during her years with Morris, the past few months in her grandfather's loving home, and her acceptance by the caring community of Hope Springs, had restored and strengthened that faith. She would not doubt again, no matter how difficult life became.

Turning around in the road, she walked back the way she had come with renewed resolve. No matter what her uncle said or did, she would turn the other cheek and give him the care he needed, even if she couldn't do it with a glad heart.

On her walk back, she noticed the Christmas decorations on the houses and lawns along the road that she had been too upset to see before. A huge blow-up snowman and an equally large Santa adorned one yard while a second house had only a row of red lights around the porch. She and her sisters had enjoyed the few times they were allowed to go into town during the Christmas season. The lights and decorations were pretty, but they didn't hold the true meaning of the season. This year, she would try hard to make her heart worthy of the gift God had given the world on that first Christmas Day. His only Son.

She reached the clinic just as the van returned. Arles got out and gave her a big smile. "Grandma Coblentz was sure happy to see her grandkids. It's the best part of my job, bringing families together. I like it when it's for weddings and Christmas, but I don't much care for carrying folks to funerals. Still, even death has its place in our lives. It brings us together, too. How is that poor cat?"

"The vet was still working on her when I stepped out."

"I hope we can get going soon. The weather report is calling for central Ohio to get heavy snow. It could be a humdinger of a storm. I'd sure like to stay ahead of it." He held open the clinic door and she walked in.

Just as they entered, the vet came out carrying a cardboard box with rows of round holes along the sides. She set the container on the chair beside Marianne and opened the top. Everyone but Morris crowded around to look.

Christmas lay curled up sleeping. The cat had a bandage around her head that left her good ear protruding through a slit in the material. The side of her neck had been shaved. A half dozen dark stitches were visible in the pink skin.

The vet held out a bottle of pills to Greta. "I've given her some sedation. She should sleep for a while. When she wakes up, I want you to give her one of these three times a day. It's an antibiotic. Keep the stitches clean and dry. Watch for signs of infection. If she starts scratching at it, cover it with a dressing. I gave her a flea treatment, too. She needed it. Give her water, but don't give her any food for a few hours. Do you have anything to feed her?"

Greta shook her head. The doctor left the room and returned with a second cardboard pet carrier. "I've put some kitty litter and a couple of pouches of cat food in here. It should be enough to last a few days. I think she'll be fine."

"Never seen a cat wearing a bonnet before. She looks almost Amish," Arles said with a chuckle.

Greta had to admit he was right. The only thing the cat's head covering was missing to make it more bonnetlike was the ribbons. After settling the bill, Greta handed the box to Marianne. It looked for a moment as if the girl would refuse to carry it, but the cat meowed pitifully from inside.

Marianne took the box and set it on the floor. She opened the top. Reaching in, she petted the cat. "It's okay. Go back to sleep."

Arles said, "We should get on the road if we are going to make Upper Sandusky before dark. We'll stop briefly in Beaverdam for Mr. Barkman to take his walk. Hopefully, we won't have any more delays."

"Just a minute." The vet left the room and returned a few moments later with a pink cord and a small pink dog harness in her hand. "You will have to keep her on a leash when you let her out so she doesn't run off. Someone left these here. You can have them. No charge. This way you won't have to put a collar over those stitches."

"That's very kind of you," Greta said.

"It was good of you to take care of this poor little stray. I'm sure her former mistress is looking down and smiling to know that her companion has found a new family."

Toby picked up the pet carriers and they all went out to the van. Without the Coblentz family taking up most of the seats, it was much roomier. Morris climbed in first. Marianne sat behind him in the second row. She looked at Toby. "Can Christmas sit with me?"

"Sure." He put the cat on the seat beside her and the box with the supplies on the floor.

He stepped aside as Greta got in. She paused beside the seat behind Marianne, but decided to go all the way to the back so Toby could sit behind his sister. She was surprised when he came and sat down with her.

"Do you mind?" he asked.

Chapter Eight

He wants to sit with me.

A flush of pleasure made Greta smile and look down. Hopefully, he wouldn't notice she was blushing. She felt like a schoolgirl again. "I don't mind at all."

"Did your walk help?"

She glanced at him sharply. "It did."

"*Goot.* Want to talk about it?"

It was tempting but she shook her head.

"And here I expected to be entertained by your nonstop chatter." His teasing tone pulled a reluctant smile from her.

"If you want nonstop chatter, I suggest you start talking."

"I guess I'm not in the mood for it, after all." He stifled a yawn.

"You can sleep. It won't bother me."

"Are you trying to tell me I look tired?"

She tipped her head to regard him closely. "Tired? *Nee.* Haggard to the point of collapse. *Ja.*"

He chuckled again. "Sadly, that is a fair assessment."

"Shall I move up to another seat so you can stretch out?"

He settled lower, leaned his head back and closed his eyes. "I think I have forgotten how to sleep lying down. It's been so long. I just need to close my eyes for a minute. I hope Marianne isn't overdoing it. I worry about her. She doesn't have much strength."

"You stayed with your sister while she was in the hospital?"

"I had to. She got very upset if I wasn't there. There wasn't anyone else to stay with her. We hadn't yet settled into a community here or joined a new church. A few of my friends came at first, but the hospital would only allow family members into the burn unit. Our aunt wanted to come, but she has a big family to care for, and I knew it would be a hardship for her. In retrospect, I should have accepted her offer."

"Do you do that often?" Greta asked.

He opened his eyes and frowned. "Do I do what?"

"Refuse help when you need it?"

He gave her a wry smile. "Am I guilty of being prideful? I have been, but I'm learning that I can't do everything."

Greta gathered her things. "Then stretch out on this bench and take a nap. I will keep an eye on your sister and wake you if she needs anything."

He nodded his consent. Greta moved up to one of the single seats where she could keep an eye on Marianne and on Toby. He folded his long legs on the seat and pillowed his head on his coat. It wasn't long before his breathing became deep and even and she knew he was asleep.

She had never watched a man sleeping before. At least no one younger than the elders who sometimes nodded off during the long church services. The lines of strain around Toby's eyes touched a chord within her. She wanted to see them soothed away.

They didn't detract from his good looks. At leisure to study him, Greta assessed his features one by one, trying to decide why she was so attracted to him. He had a strong square jaw and lean cheeks with high cheekbones. His nose was a little too prominent, but added to the whole, it fit him. She decided his mouth was his best feature. His lips were perfectly shaped, not too full, not too thin, and they curved easily into a friendly smile. Yes, she liked his smile the best. And the small dimple it revealed in his left cheek.

His dark brown hair was fine and straight, but it was cut shorter than the traditional Amish bowl-style. Young men during their *rumspringa,* the years when they were free to try English ways and decide if they wanted to remain Amish, often adopted English hairstyles. There was nothing remotely English about his clothing. He wore dark, homemade pants, a pale blue shirt and black suspenders. Had he left his *rumspringa* behind or was he only dressing Amish because he was going to visit his Amish family?

Greta realized there was a lot about this young man that intrigued her, but it was unlikely that she would learn much on this short trip. She glanced toward his sister. Marianne was napping, too. She had wedged herself into the corner of the seat. Her head rested against the window glass.

Greta took off her coat and folded it into a bundle. Slipping in next to the child, Greta eased her coat beneath the girl's cheek without waking her. She glanced over the seat back at her uncle. He had assumed the same position. She seemed to be the only one who couldn't sleep.

Returning to her seat, she took out her needlepoint hoop and began to work. It didn't require much concentration, but the repetitive motion helped to keep her mind off her unhappy situation. The thing she regretted most was bringing her uncle into her sisters' lives again.

Lizzie with her delicate pregnancy did not need to be subjected to their uncle's cruel verbal barbs. Betsy had become a fun-loving teenager. Even their oldest sister, Clara, had come out of her shell and gained the confidence to marry a man with three children. None of them deserved to be exposed to their uncle's venom.

Greta's one consolation was that he wouldn't dare raise a hand to any of them as long as Duncan was in the house.

The dog considered them part of his flock. He would lay down his life to defend them.

The miles rolled by as she worked, glancing occasionally at the other passengers. They all slept. Christmas remained quiet in her box. Greta was tempted to open the carton and check on her, but decided against it. There was no telling what the cat would do when she sensed freedom.

Sometime later, Greta was losing the light to work by when Arles pulled off the interstate and turned into the parking lot of a fast-food restaurant adjacent to a large truck stop. Toby sat up in the back and looked around. Marianne remained asleep, but Morris sat up, too. As if on cue, the cat began to meow softly. Arles turned around in his seat. "I'm going to get something to drink. Does anyone want anything?"

Greta shook her head, as did Toby. Arles left, closing his door softly. Toby came forward to his sister's seat. Seeing her asleep, he handed Greta the pet carrier and gently lifted Marianne in his arms. Returning to the rear of the vehicle, he laid her down on the seat and covered her with his coat. She didn't rouse.

Greta retrieved her coat and slipped it on. She opened the box and lifted the cat out. Toby came forward. "We should put the lead on her before we take her outside." He spoke softly so as not to wake his sister.

"I was thinking the same thing. Can you get it from the box under the seat?"

He extracted the pink harness and cord. "If you hold her, I think I can get it on without too much trouble. Let's hope she's still groggy enough to be cooperative."

"Be careful that she doesn't bite or scratch you," Greta cautioned.

"I'll try. I've never harnessed a cat before."

"Me, either," Greta said with a smothered giggle.

Christmas allowed herself to be buckled in with a minimum of fuss. Greta looked at Toby with relief. "Open the door and let's see how she does."

"It's a bunch of foolishness," Morris said, but Greta noticed he was waiting patiently to get out.

Toby opened the door and Greta stepped down with the cat in her arms. Christmas seemed content to stay where she was.

"Goot katz," Greta crooned, stroking the uninjured side of her neck. Morris walked past her without comment.

Toby got out and stood beside Greta. "Put her on the ground and let's see what she does."

Greta, holding tight to the lead, set the cat on her feet. Christmas lay down on the pavement, showing no inclination to move.

Toby folded his arms and rocked back on his heels. "I was expecting a little more action."

"So was I. Maybe she has worn a leash before and knows how to behave on one."

"Anything is possible. See if she will walk with you."

Greta tugged on the lead. "Come, Christmas. Let's go for a walk."

Christmas refused to budge. Morris, who was standing nearby said, "Put some water where she can see it."

"Couldn't hurt. I'll get some." Toby headed toward the restaurant.

Greta was still trying unsuccessfully to coax the cat to take a few steps while her uncle walked nearby when Toby returned. He carried a plastic bowl and a bottle of water. Kneeling, he poured the water into the bowl and pushed it toward the cat. Christmas inched forward and began to lap at his offering, slowly at first, but then more eagerly. When she finished drinking her fill, she sat up and began licking her paws.

"It's a *goot* sign. She's strong," Morris said as he got back in the van.

First, he called it foolishness to care for the cat. Then he was offering helpful suggestions. Greta wasn't sure what to make of his comments. Was he concerned about the animal? If so, it would be the first time she had known him to show compassion toward another living creature. Was he changing? Was it possible?

She had to remember that anything was possible with God.

Arles came out of the restaurant with a soft drink in his hand. "Let's go, folks. We'll be stopping in Upper Sandusky for the night. It's only an hour from here."

Christmas went back into her box without protest. They were soon on the road. It was full dark by the time they entered the outskirts of the city. Toby spoke for the first time since leaving Beaverdam. "Greta, can Marianne room with you tonight?"

"Of course."

"*Danki.* I don't like the idea of her staying in a room by herself even if I am next door."

"I understand." She glanced forward.

"Do you think your uncle would mind sharing a room with me?" Toby asked.

"I was hoping you would offer. I don't like the idea of him staying alone, either, but I have no idea how he will feel about it."

"Perhaps he won't mind when I mention splitting the cost of the room."

"Knowing my uncle, that will appeal to him."

"It won't hurt to ask." Toby moved to the front of the van and sat down beside Morris.

As it turned out, Greta was right. Morris agreed to share a room and split the cost. Knowing there would be someone close by if her uncle had difficulty would make it much easier for her to face the coming night.

When Toby returned to sit by her, she gave him the list

of medicines the nurse had shared with her and told him which ones Morris needed to take before bed and in the morning. Then, she explained how he was to use the nitro pills. "Is this too much of a burden?" she asked.

"I can manage. If not, you will be close by."

"That's true."

As they rolled through the city, Greta gazed out the window in wonder, feeling like a kid again. Christmas lights and decorations adorned houses and businesses. Everywhere, colored lights painted the night with red, green, gold and blue hues.

Marianne woke when they stopped at a traffic light. Sitting up, she looked around. "Where are we? Where is Christmas?"

The child's voice was a little stronger. Greta patted the box. "She's right here with me. She has been sleeping, too. We are in Upper Sandusky. This is where we're stopping for the night. Look at all the decorations. See the snowflakes hanging over the street. Aren't they beautiful?"

"Ah, they are *wunderbarr.*"

"I think so, too," Toby said.

The child pressed her face to the window. "The *Englisch* sure like to fancy things up."

"Indeed they do," Greta agreed, sharing a grin with Toby.

Arles pulled into the parking lot of a motel and went inside to arrange for their rooms. Greta gathered her things and the cat carrier.

"Are you hungry?" Toby asked after they got out of the vehicle.

"A little," Marianne replied.

"I see a pizza place across the street. What kind would you like?"

"Pepperoni."

He smiled at her. "I should have remembered. Greta, what about you?"

"The same, only with extra cheese."

"Morris, would you like to share a pizza pie with us?"

"Not unless you want to kill me. I'm supposed to watch my diet carefully. Pizza is not on it."

Greta wanted to shake him for being rude, but she quelled the urge. "What would you like to eat, *Onkel?*"

"I'd like a thick juicy steak, but my doctor says I must eat more salads."

Toby said, "That should be easy enough. The sign says they have a salad bar. Once we get checked in, I'll go get our supper and we can eat in our rooms. How does that sound?"

"Fine as long as I can lie down. Greta, fetch my bags." He walked toward the motel lobby.

Greta closed her eyes and clamped her jaws together.

"Take a deep breath," Toby said softly in her ear.

She blew out a long breath. "I prayed for patience. I guess the Lord thinks I need more practice using what little I have."

"I can get his bags."

"*Danki,* but I can manage them." They walked to the rear of the van, and Toby opened the compartment for her. She pulled out her uncle's suitcases and her own small bag. Toby took the suitcases from her.

Arles came out of the lobby and stopped beside them. "I'm sorry folks, but I'm afraid I've got some bad news."

Chapter Nine

"What sort of bad news?" Greta asked.

Arles, looking apologetic, addressed Marianne. "I'm sorry, honey, this motel doesn't allow pets in the rooms. I didn't know we would have a cat with us when I made the reservation. I'm afraid she'll have to stay in the van tonight or we will have to find another motel. I checked us in, but if you want to try somewhere else, they'll give us a refund."

Morris pounded his cane on the pavement. "I'm tired. I want to go to my room. The rest of you can go somewhere else, but I'm not letting that stupid cat keep me up any longer. Bunch of nonsense bringing that thing along, anyway."

Marianne huddled against Greta's side. "Christmas won't like staying in the van alone. She'll be scared."

"We don't have a choice," Toby said.

"You don't like her because she's ugly." Marianne buried her face in Greta's skirt.

Greta cupped the back of her head. "That's not true and you know it. Your brother is right. We can't take Christmas into our room. She will have to stay out here."

"*Nee.* She can't. I don't want her to be afraid."

Greta lifted Marianne's chin so the frowning girl would look at her. "Until today, Christmas was sleeping in alleys and under porches. I'm sure she will be happy to be safe and warm in the van."

Marianne's scowl faded. "I didn't think of that."

"In an alley is where she belongs," Morris grumped.

Ignoring him, Toby knelt beside Marianne. "I'll come out and check on her during the night to make sure she's okay."

Marianne looked doubtful. "You promise?"

"I promise. Let's get you settled, and then I'll fix up a place in the back of the van for Christmas to sleep."

"Your rooms are down this way. I got them next to each other." Arles said. Marianne and Morris followed him leaving Greta and Toby to deal with the luggage.

"Crisis averted." Toby hefted his duffel bag and Morris's suitcases.

"For now," Greta agreed.

Arles unlocked the door and said, "This one is for you and Marianne, Greta. I hope it's okay." There were two full-size beds in the room along with a dresser and a television.

"It looks fine." Greta walked in and put her suitcase down. Arles walked on and unlocked the next door. Morris went inside without a word.

Toby waited for Marianne to object to the arrangements. She was used to having him sleep in the same room while she was in the hospital. He put his duffel bag on the bed and pulled out her things.

Marianne looked around the room. She walked close to his side and whispered, "Where are you going to sleep?"

"Where do you think?" He waited for her to make the connection. She knew. She just didn't like the idea.

"You can't sleep in here. There's no bed for you."

"That's right. Now that you are out of the hospital, I won't be sharing your room anymore. I'll be right next door, though. You and Greta get to share tonight. She has agreed to keep an eye on you, and I have agreed to keep an eye on her uncle. He's been sick, too and he needs some-one to look after him."

"What if I get scared?"

"Honey, Greta will be with you."

Marianne clenched her hands together. "What if I need you?"

"If you need me, I want you to knock on the wall like this." He rapped the wall over her headboard three times. "I'll come right over."

"I guess that will be okay."

"What a brave girl you are. Greta, take good care of her."

"Don't worry, I will." She closed the door behind him, and smiled at Marianne. "Now it's time for some girl fun. This is like having a sleepover."

After settling in the small but clean motel room, Greta unpacked her night things. Even though they were inside, Marianne didn't remove her oversize black bonnet. Greta decided not to push the issue knowing when Marianne felt comfortable with her, she would. Toby delivered the pizza thirty minutes later. After Greta closed the door behind him again, she turned to Marianne. "Shall we watch tele-vision while we eat?"

Marianne's mouth dropped open. "Can we?"

Since neither of them were baptized members of the faith, Greta knew it wasn't strictly forbidden, just frowned upon. She would make sure they watched something ap-propriate for a child of ten. "I won't tell if you won't tell."

Eyes round as silver dollars, Marianne said, "I won't."

Greta turned to the black box on the dresser and real-ized she was at a disadvantage. She looked at Marianne. "Do you know how to turn it on?"

"Sure. The nurses at the hospital showed me. Find the remote."

They opened drawers until they discovered the device

and then sat cross-legged on the bed with the pizza box between them. They giggled together at the silly commercials, sat aghast at some of the others and thoroughly enjoyed a movie about a young girl and her horse. For Greta, being with Marianne was a lot like being with her sisters. It made her miss them. She would be happy to reach home tomorrow.

Later, after saying their prayers, Greta was prepared to turn out the lights when she noticed that Marianne still hadn't removed her bonnet. Greta flipped the switch and lay down. Although she was tired, she found she wasn't sleepy. Apparently, Marianne wasn't either after her long nap.

"Are you afraid of the dark?" Marianne asked.

Greta detected an edge of fear in the child's voice. "*Nee,* I'm not. The Lord tells us not to be afraid for He is always with us. I'm sure that means even in the dark. I remember how my sisters and I would often exchange confidences in our bedroom at night. Being in the dark somehow made it easier to talk about the boy I liked or about something that happened at school. Do you like school?"

"I liked school in Pennsylvania. I didn't like it in Indiana."

"I imagine that's because all your friends were in Pennsylvania. Did you make new friends in Indiana?"

"Only one. Her name was Mary Beth. She came to see me in the hospital."

"That was kind of her."

"It was the first day they took off my bandages. She cried when she saw what I looked like."

"That must have been very hard for you."

"I told her not to come back. She didn't."

"I'm sorry. But your brother stayed with you. Did that make you feel better?"

"I don't want to talk about it."

Should she let it go, or press the issue? Greta decided to press gently. "Talking about things can help us feel better."

"Toby cried sometimes, too. He thinks I'm ugly the same way Mary Beth did."

"He doesn't. He loves you, and he sees your good heart."

There was a long pause. Greta thought Marianne might have fallen asleep, but she finally spoke. "I wish he hadn't made us move to Indiana."

"My goodness, however did he do that?"

"He kept telling *Daed* about all the jobs that were there. He talked about the money they could make together. *Mamm* and I didn't want to go, but Toby talked *Daed* into it. If we had stayed in Pennsylvania, they would still be alive."

"I can see why you feel that way."

"You can?" Marianne sounded surprised.

"Of course. One thing led to the other, didn't it? Do you think Toby wanted your parents to die?"

"Nee!"

Greta heard the shock in Marianne's tone and she knew she was making her point. "I don't think so, either. Do you think he knew when he talked about better wages that it would lead to their deaths?"

"Nee, but we should have stayed where we were. We were happy there."

"Your father couldn't find work. Did that make him happy?"

"He worried a lot about it. He didn't like asking the church for help although *Mamm* said he should."

"It sounds to me like your brother and your father were a lot alike. Marianne, God chose to bring your mother and father to heaven. Toby had nothing to do with it. I know this has been a very sad time for you, but you do understand that, don't you?"

When the child didn't answer, Greta said, "Good night, Marianne. Sleep well."

Several more minutes of silence passed until Marianne said, "I knocked over the lamp that started the fire."

Oh, you poor child.

Greta slipped out of bed, sat beside Marianne and took hold of her hand. "It was an accident. You didn't mean for something bad to happen. It wasn't your fault any more than it was Toby's fault."

"I couldn't get out. I screamed for *Daed* to come get me."

"Someone got you out. Was it your brother?"

"My clothes were on fire. *Daed* broke down the door. He threw a blanket over me and carried me outside. Then he ran back to get *Mamm* and Toby. I screamed and screamed but they never came out. I was all alone. The house fell down, and they still didn't come."

No wonder she was fearful of having her brother out of her sight. Greta lifted the child in her arms. "God was with you. He was with your mother and father, too. We are never alone. It's okay to be sad and scared. God understands. The wonderful thing about God's plan for us is that we are only on earth for a little time. Once we reach heaven, we will spend an eternity with the ones we love in everlasting joy. Every tear we cried will be wiped away. So we must live a good life and keep God in our thoughts always so we can join Him there."

"Don't tell Toby what I did."

"It's not my secret to share, but you need to tell him."

"He might hate me."

"He won't."

"How do you know?"

"Because I think he has a good heart, too. Can you go to sleep now?"

"I think so."

"Goot." Greta tucked her in and returned to her bed. It had been a long and eventful day, but if anything she said helped Marianne, it was worth the trip.

When Toby opened his eyes, it was already light outside. Surprised that he had slept so long, he glanced at the other bed. Morris was already up and gone. Dressing quickly, Toby opened the motel room door and surveyed the parking lot. The sky was heavily overcast with a cold north wind whipping across the pavement. There were a dozen cars lined up in front of the building, but there was no sign of the elderly man. Toby heard the door to Greta's room open and he winced. "Great. Some caretaker I turned out to be."

Greta stepped out, caught sight of him and smiled brightly. Just as quickly, she blushed a becoming shade of pink and looked down. Did that mean she liked him? He hoped so because he liked her. Marianne came out behind her with her nightclothes in her hand. She raced to his side and threw her arms around him.

He smiled warmly at Greta. "Good morning."

"Good cold morning." She pulled her coat more tightly around her. "Where are Arles and my uncle?"

"I think they may be having a free cup of coffee in the lobby. I'll go see."

He wanted to check there before he admitted he had no idea where her uncle was. He prayed the ill old man was all right.

Arles was sitting alone at a small table with a foam cup in front of him reading the paper when Toby checked the small room. "Arles, have you seen Morris?"

"Mr. Barkman? No."

That wasn't what Toby wanted to hear.

Arles took a sip of coffee and then said, "The van is unlocked. Can I have my spare key back?"

"Sure." Toby fished it from his pocket and handed it over. Arles had given it to him so he could check on the cat through the night.

Toby left him and stopped at the front desk, but the clerk on duty hadn't seen Morris, either. Toby paid his bill. When he came out of the building, he saw Greta and Marianne standing beside the open door of the van. It looked as if Marianne was sobbing. He broke into a run.

Chapter Ten

"Marianne, what's wrong?" Toby asked when he reached her side.

"Christmas is gone," she managed between sobs.

Toby looked at Greta for an explanation. She said, "She's not in her box."

"She was there when I checked on her at two last night. Maybe she's hiding under the seats, or maybe she got in back with the luggage somehow."

They searched the interior of the van to no avail. The cat wasn't inside. Toby carefully lifted the hatch to the luggage compartment, prepared to close it if he saw the animal. Nothing moved. He raised the lid higher and checked behind the bags.

Greta paused with her hand on a black suitcase she was about to move aside. "This is my uncle's."

"He must've loaded them himself. I didn't do it. He was already gone when I woke up. I'm afraid I didn't keep a very good eye on him," Toby admitted.

"Oh, dear."

The look on her face said she was thinking the same thing he was. "Do you think he let the cat out by accident when he put his bags in?" he asked.

She shook her head. "I doubt it was an accident. He wasn't happy having her along."

"There she is!" Marianne took off toward the rear of

the building. Morris was coming around the corner from the back. Christmas, wearing her white bonnet bandage and pink harness, walked beside him. He had her leash in his hand. The cat lay down and offered her tummy for scratching as Marianne reached her.

"It seems we judged your uncle unfairly." Toby said, happy to see everyone was in good shape.

Greta crossed her arms. A faint scowl put a crease between her brows. "It appears that I did. This time."

Toby wondered again at the cause of the tension between Greta and her uncle. She seemed determined to think the worst of him.

Greta couldn't believe her eyes. Her uncle had taken the cat for a walk. Why? What did he hope to gain? Did he believe the cat would warn him of an impending attack? In that case, she could understand why he would take a stroll with Christmas. She knew he hadn't done it solely for the cat's welfare.

"Thank you for taking Christmas for a walk." Marianne accepted the lead from Morris and picked up the cat.

"She has done her business. Perhaps now we can get going."

His gruff tone made it sound as if he didn't care about the cat, but Greta saw him pet Christmas briefly before walking to the van and getting in.

"Your uncle likes Christmas," Marianne said with a smile.

"It would appear that he does," Greta agreed, reluctant to disillusion the child.

Toby ran a hand over the faint stubble on his cheek. "I've already checked out, but I still need to finish getting ready. I don't normally oversleep like this. Here comes Arles. Don't let him leave without me."

As Toby disappeared inside his room, Greta paid her bill

and returned to the van. Arles was already in the driver's seat, impatient to get going. "I've got breakfast for everyone." He handed back a small white sack that contained an assortment of bagels and cans of juice.

Her uncle and Marianne each chose something without complaint. Greta took what was left and headed to the rear seat. As he had the day before, Toby joined her. He had a small patch of tissue stuck to his chin. He had barely taken his seat before Arles had them on the road again.

Toby nodded toward Marianne. "My sister looks much more rested today."

"So do you," Greta said, studying his handsome face.

"No longer haggard to the point of collapse?" he asked with a teasing grin.

"I would say bright-eyed and bushy-tailed."

"Taking a two-minute shower and shave will do that to a fellow." He pulled the bit of tissue free and turned his chin toward her. "Has it stopped bleeding?"

"*Ja*, it looks like you will live." She handed him the sack. "Arles splurged on breakfast for all of us. Bagels and juice."

"For the price he's charging for this trip, he should." Taking the sack, he peered inside. "Did you have yours?"

"Not yet. I didn't know if you wanted the blueberry or the raisin-cinnamon one."

He handed the bag back to her. "Pick which one you like and I'll take what's left."

She hesitated and then leaned forward. "Marianne, does your brother like blueberries or raisins better?"

She looked over the seat. "He hates raisins."

"*Danki*, that's what I needed to know." Greta extracted the cinnamon-raisin bagel and handed the sack to him.

Taking it, he said, "I would have eaten it if you wanted the blueberry one."

"I'm not fond of blueberries except in pie. Apple juice or orange juice?" She held up the cans.

"You pick."

"I asked first."

"Apple," he said quickly.

She pulled both cans to her chest. "Oh, that's the one I wanted."

"Then give me the orange."

"But I like that one, too."

His smile widened making his eyes sparkle with amusement. "I don't really care which one you want. You can have both."

Greta held out the apple juice. "Since I told you to pick, you can have it."

"I'll share with you," he offered.

"I was just teasing you. I like orange juice better."

"Sometimes, women are too complex for me."

Greta observed her uncle turn around and speak with Marianne as the van rolled down the highway. She couldn't hear what they were saying, but they seemed to be having an animated conversation. She cast a covert glance at the man beside her. He, too, was watching her uncle and his sister intently.

She liked Toby, far more than she should after knowing him for such a brief period of time. There was something about being cocooned together in the back of the van that made his companionship comfortable. That, and she found him attractive.

She liked the way his smile curved up one cheek and then the other to reveal a full-blown grin with a dimple on his left cheek. He had a keen mind and a good sense of humor, and she would never see him again after today. The thought was sad but liberating. She didn't have to pretend to be something she wasn't.

"You're not very close to your uncle, are you?"

His blunt question startled her. She opened her mouth to deny it, but hadn't she just told herself she didn't have to pretend? It didn't matter what Toby Yoder thought of her or of her uncle. She turned in her seat so she could face him. "We're not close."

"Were you ever?" His gaze was fixed on his sister.

"*Nee,* we never have been. I tried very hard to make him like me when I was Marianne's age, but it didn't matter what I did. It's a shame, because we are all the family that he has left."

She hadn't been able to win her uncle's love. Was the fault his, or was there something wrong with her? It seemed that she was always the one who sparked his anger. Anger that spilled over onto her sisters, too.

"I can assure you that I care deeply about my sister."

Greta gave Toby a tentative smile. "I have seen that, too, yet something is wrong between you."

"She is terrified if I'm out of her sight, but she blames me for the death of our parents. I don't know how to help her accept that it was God's will."

"Have you accepted it?"

He turned to study her intently. "Are you always so blunt?"

She looked away, aware that she had stepped over the line in questioning his faith. "I apologize."

"Don't be sorry. I know only God has the power of life and death. I believe that. For some reason, God wanted my folks to be with Him sooner than I would've liked. He spared my sister. For that I am truly grateful, but I don't know why He left me unscathed."

"Perhaps He knew you needed to be strong for Marianne."

"Perhaps, but I don't think I'm strong enough."

"You must not give up on her. Eventually, her heart

will heal just as the burns on her face and neck will heal. If you weren't home, why is it that you blame yourself?"

"You don't leave any stone unturned, do you?"

"You can tell me to mind my own business."

"Maybe I should."

"Maybe you should. Or maybe you should talk about it. Things that hide in the dark frighten us until we shine a light into that dark corner. Then we see that there was nothing to be frightened of, after all." She was better at giving advice than she was at living it.

"Is it really that easy?"

"Give it a try."

He drew a deep breath. "My father and I worked at a small furniture factory outside of Quarryville, Pennsylvania. He was a master carver. God gave him a great talent. He taught me a lot, but I never had his gift. I didn't try to love and understand the wood the way he did. The owner was an *Englisch* fellow. He liked to hire the Amish because he didn't have to pay us as much as *Englisch* workers. When the economy took a turn for the worse, he closed up shop and we were without work. Things got very difficult."

"Times have been tough for many Amish and *Englisch* families."

"I had a friend who had moved to Indiana. He was working in one of the RV factories. I couldn't believe the wages he was being paid. He said he had work for all of us. I convinced my parents to move to Fort Wayne. It wasn't easy, but finally we had no choice. It was move or become a drain on my mother's family who were helping to support us. Father couldn't stand that."

He fell silent. Greta could see he was struggling to find the right words. "You were trying to help your family. There is no shame in that."

"I know. I did think I had helped. We found an old

farmhouse to rent, and *Daed* and I both got jobs. The pay was good. The work wasn't hard, but my father hated it. He said it had no soul. He wanted to move back and start carving again."

"And you didn't."

"I was too busy enjoying having money for the first time in my life. I was in my *rumspringa*. I had friends. We went to parties. We went to movies. It was great. The more my parents hinted that I should join the church, the more I refused to listen. I wasn't home the night of the fire. I wasn't there to save them."

"What would have happened to Marianne if you had perished, too?"

"I want to believe that I was spared so that I could take care of her. More than anything, I want her to be the happy girl who used to come running to see me when I stopped in to visit. But I'm afraid all she will ever see is the self-ish brother who brought disaster down on her."

Greta reached out and covered his hand with hers. "She's young. Time will heal both of you."

"I know one thing. I'm never leaving her again. My *rumspringa* is over. We will have a simple Amish life among my mother's people."

"Goot."

He gave her fingers a squeeze. "You have a talent for this. For helping."

"Have I helped you?" She tried to ignore the thrill that raced through her at his touch.

"I think so."

"Then I'm happy."

When they reached the next hourly stop, Arles pulled over at the edge of a small park not far from the highway. Marianne got out with Christmas in her harness and put the cat down. The cat tentatively began to explore the side-walk and nearby grass. Morris walked beside Marianne as she made her way to a wooden bench that overlooked an ice-rimmed pond. The two sat down together with the cat between their feet. Christmas crouched low, her gaze focused on a dozen ducks floating in a stretch of open water in front of her.

Toby stood beside Greta. "My sister is doing better now that she has something else to focus on."

Greta folded her arms self-consciously. "It's often the case that our troubles seem less important when we are helping someone else. I said I would take Christmas home, but I think she may do better to stay with your sister. Would that be possible?"

"It's very kind of you to offer. I think Marianne would love that. It looks as though there is a path around the lake, would you care to walk with me?"

Greta's gaze flew to his face. She bit the corner of her lip. For an Amish man to invite a single woman to go walking with him implied a desire for more than friendship. Did he mean it that way?

Should she accept?

Chapter Eleven

Greta agonized over how to answer Toby.

His expression slowly changed from hopeful to puzzled. Why was she stalling? She wanted to go.

A walk in the park was a lot less intimate than sitting together in the backseat of the van. It wasn't as if the request meant anything special. It didn't. It was a gesture of kindness to a fellow traveler. She could accept that.

"A walk would be nice."

Nice? There was an understatement. Maybe exciting or awesome, but not plain old nice.

"*Goot.*" He began walking, and she fell into step beside him. Almost close enough to touch. When his hand did accidently brush hers, she stopped breathing for a second. Oh, being with him was so much more than nice.

It was amazing how freeing it was to know she didn't have to watch every word with this young man. She could be as outspoken as Lizzie or as serene as Clara. He would never know the difference. She didn't have to be plain, *goot* Greta the mouse who tended the gardens and the animals.

They walked slowly, neither one of them in a hurry to get around the little lake. A life-size nativity had been set up beside the path where a backdrop of cedar trees provided a windbreak. The wooden cutouts of the Christ child, Mary, Joseph, the stable, a shepherd and several of his flock were all painted bright white. Against the deep green of the trees, it made a pretty scene.

"Do those sheep look familiar?" Toby asked with a teasing grin.

"My grandfather raises a much fatter breed," she answered struggling to keep a straight face. His chuckle was music to her ears. She would never grow tired of hearing it or of seeing the dimple that appeared in his left cheek when he smiled.

Farther along the path was a gaily painted gingerbread house from which Santa and his reindeer appeared to be taking off down a runway flanked by five-foot-tall lollipops and candy canes. The wind was chilly, but Greta didn't mind. She was often outdoors on the farm in all kinds of weather. Besides, she was tired of being cooped up in the van, and Toby's company was keeping her warm.

As they walked farther along, he grew serious, pushing his hands in his pockets. "I couldn't help but notice the animosity between you and your uncle. I know it's none of my business, but if you would like to talk about it I could listen."

"You are turning my words back on me, aren't you?" she asked, casting him a sidelong glance.

"I feel better for having talked about my troubles. You should try it."

She looked straight ahead. "I don't wish to speak ill of him."

"The truth is the truth. It is neither good nor ill."

He was right, but could she tell her story without revealing how poorly she practiced her faith? Without revealing how frightened she was of becoming the mouse of a person her uncle had made her.

Toby waited calmly. He didn't press her. He was such a kind man. Perhaps sharing her fears would make them less. And why not? She was unlikely to see Toby again after today.

She drew a deep breath. "After our parents died, *Onkel* Morris took us in. I have three sisters. Outwardly, it seemed a kind and generous thing to do. Behind closed doors, that was not the case."

"Your uncle treated you unkindly? I've noticed he's not a likable fellow."

"It was worse than unkindness. He was cruel to us." She glanced at Toby but saw only interest and compassion in his eyes, not judgment. She looked down. "He beat us often."

"I'm sorry. I had no idea. No wonder you seem so reserved around him."

"I won't bore you with the details, but eventually he tried to force my sister Clara to marry a terrible man. We were powerless to stop it until my brave sister Lizzie ran away and found our estranged grandfather. She secured a place for all of us and then sent money to a friend to help us leave. We did so without my uncle's consent on the morning of Clara's wedding day. Morris was humiliated, as was the man who wished to marry her. They came after us and tried to force us to return. God, in his greatness, sent a wonderful dog named Duncan to foil their plans."

"God is good."

"He is indeed."

"What of your family now?"

"Two of my sisters are happily wed to kind and generous men. My third sister may soon follow in their footsteps."

"And you?"

"I have no plans to wed."

"Because you haven't met the right fellow," he said with a knowing smile.

"It's not just that. I'm not sure what I'm going to do with

my life." How could she be a good wife and mother if she had not forgiveness in her heart?

"I don't understand."

She managed a wry smile. "I'm not surprised. I'm considering going on with my schooling. I'm thinking about becoming a counselor and working with abused women."

Toby stopped walking and looked at her in surprise. "You mean leave the Amish?"

Toby was stunned. He didn't know Greta well, but she didn't seem like someone willing to discard her Amish upbringing. During his *rumspringa,* he'd met a few Amish girls who were anxious to escape their restrictive lives. They were easy to spot. They dressed *Englisch* every chance they got. Some of them smoked and drank. A few he knew had even experimented with drugs. He didn't sense that restlessness in Greta.

Maybe it was because she wasn't looking to escape. She wanted to help others. He admired that.

"Are you shocked?" she asked.

"A little." He looked at her through different eyes. Until a moment ago, he had been wondering if they could maintain their budding relationship over a long distance. It was possible. His cousin Marvin had written to a girl he met at a wedding in Wisconsin and eventually married her after many letters and a few long-distance trips. They were happy together. But a relationship with someone ready to leave the Amish had never been on Toby's horizon. He'd enjoyed his *rumspringa,* but he always intended to be baptized and raise an Amish family.

"What type of schooling would that require? Perhaps your bishop could give you a special dispensation if the need is great in your church."

"I do not believe it would be granted. Child and spouse abuse occur in every walk of life, even among Christian people, but I don't think we Amish are as aware of it as the *Englisch* are. We tend to keep such things hidden if they occur to avoid interference by outsiders. We forgive unconditionally, but I fear we do not treat the cause of the problem. I would have to finish high school and go on to college to eventually become a counselor."

"That would take many years of study. Is this something you have set your mind on?" he asked. Such a decision could not be an easy one.

"I've given it a lot of thought, but after this trip I realized I may not be ready."

"Why do you say that?"

She started walking again. "I realize that I haven't forgiven my uncle for his abuse. I'm not sure I can help other women find forgiveness and heal if I can't find it in myself."

"But we must forgive. It is God's commandment to us."

"I've tried. I thought I had come to grips with it, but I'm still so angry with him. I didn't even want to accompany him on this trip. I did so because my youngest sister was the only other person who could come, and she is too young to make this trip alone. I thought after his heart attack that he might have changed. I was hoping… I don't know what I was hoping for. Forgiveness, some sign of remorse for the way he treated us in the past."

"Reconciliation," Toby said softly.

"Perhaps," she agreed.

"Forgiveness is one-sided, Greta. We can forgive someone without them being aware of it. It is simply between us and God. The other person doesn't need to have any part in that act. When we want forgiveness *and* a chance for a new relationship, we are really looking for reconciliation."

"Maybe that is what I want. He's family, after all. No one should be alone at the end of their life."

They walked in silence until they reached a small footbridge that spanned the stream flowing into the pond. Painted white, the wooden railings were adorned with swags of evergreen boughs tied on with large red bows. The scent of pine and the sound of rushing water filled the air. Greta stopped and leaned on the railing. Toby did the same. He propped his forearms on the wood and watched the water flowing between the icy banks beneath them as it raced to the pond and vanished under the ice.

He and Greta were journeying toward their destinations, too. Unlike the water below, they weren't headed in the same direction. What might have happened between them if they were going the same way? If she wanted to remain Amish? If he didn't have to think of his sister first? If they didn't live hundreds of miles apart?

They were questions without answers. None of that really mattered. They would go their separate ways soon. All he had been granted was a few hours with this amazing woman.

Greta glanced toward Toby and found him watching her. There was a soft light in his eyes, a kind of sadness, but something else, too. She clasped her hands tightly together to keep from reaching out to touch him. "It's strange. I find myself telling you things I have not shared with anyone else."

"I know it has taken a great deal of courage for you to tell me these things."

"You have made it easy," she said softly, hoping he understood how much his kindness meant to her.

"I suppose it's easy because we won't see each other after today. Or maybe it's because we have been shut in the back of that van together for *hours* and *hours*."

It might be part of the reason, but it wasn't the entire reason. There was something special about this young man. He touched a chord in her that she never knew existed. As much as she wanted to reach home, she didn't want their journey together to end. Once she reached the farm, she would be plain, *goot* Greta again.

She glanced at him from the corner of her eye. "It hasn't been that bad, has it?"

He smiled sweetly. *"Nee,* it hasn't been bad at all."

A thrill tumbled across her heart. She looked away hoping to hide how much she wanted him to take her hand or drape his arm over her shoulder.

Foolish wishes.

Across the small lake, she saw her uncle and Marianne heading back to the van. Greta didn't want to return. She wanted to stay here, on this little footbridge and spend hours with Toby. She wanted to learn everything there was to know about the man beside her. She already knew that he was kind, that he loved his sister deeply and that he was wise beyond his years.

He looked up. "It's starting to snow."

The wind swirled around them, driving a few cold flakes against her cheeks. It was God's way of telling her that she could not stay here. Her life could not stand still. She had to move on. And that meant parting from Toby.

"We should get back to the van," he said, but he didn't move.

"All good things must end," she said quietly.

"This is a good thing, isn't it?" He was gazing out at the pond, but the moment he spoke, he looked directly at her and she knew he was talking about them. She read the truth in his eyes. He felt the same compelling connection that made her long for more time together, but it wasn't to be.

"You have been a marvelous traveling companion, Toby Yoder."

He smiled sadly. "You, too, Greta Barkman."

There was no reason to prolong the inevitable. Greta pushed away from the rail and started walking with Toby close beside her. Neither of them said anything until they reached the van.

Marianne and Arles were already inside. Christmas was meowing and tugging at her lead, struggling to get out of Marianne's arms. Greta looked around. "Where is my uncle?"

"I think Christmas was annoying him. She kept pawing at him. He said he needed to stretch his legs a little more. He went that way." Marianne pointed toward the path that led through an arbor set between thick stands of shrubs.

"We need to get going," Arles said impatiently.

"I'll go get him."

Greta walked the way Marianne had pointed. The snowflakes were growing thicker and larger. She blinked away the ones that stuck to her lashes and picked up her pace. As she passed through the arbor, she stumbled to a halt and stood frozen in place as she stared at her uncle's crumpled figure lying on the ground.

Chapter Twelve

She couldn't move.

All the years of cringing and avoiding Morris, of trying not to attract his attention, trying and failing not to trigger his wrath, all those memories and more put a wall in front of Greta. She didn't have to help him.

Even as the thought crossed her mind, she knew it wasn't true.

She did have to help. If she didn't, she would be no better than he was. He did not get to win. He did not get to make her into his own image.

She rushed across the brown grass and knelt at his side. He was breathing. She gently rolled him onto his back and loosened his collar. Was it enough? What else could she do? Should she scream for help or run back to the van?

He moaned. She took his hand between her own. "*Onkel,* can you hear me? What do I do?"

"Another pill," he whispered.

She checked his pockets but the vial was gone. She looked around and saw it lying near his feet. She grabbed it, quickly shook a pill into her hand and put it under his tongue. After a minute, his breathing grew easier.

"I'm going to go get help." She rushed through the arbor and saw Toby waiting for her beside the van.

The instant he caught sight of her he broke into a run toward her. "What's wrong?"

"Morris has had another attack."

Toby rushed past her, and she hurried to keep up with him. When Toby reached Morris, he gently lifted his head. "Do you need an ambulance?"

"*Nee,* I don't want to die in a hospital. Help me to my feet. I can walk now."

She and Toby helped Morris stand. He wavered for a moment, then straightened. "It appears God is not ready to take me. Here comes the child. Don't alarm her."

"What's wrong?" Marianne asked as she rushed to Morris's side.

He laid a hand on her shoulder. "I walked too far, and I needed a short rest, but I'm ready to go back to the van now."

"I'll help you. You can lean on me," she said.

Her uncle did something that Greta had never seen. He smiled, but there was a faraway look in his eyes. "*Danki,* Miriam. You have always been my *goot* little helper."

"My name is Marianne, but you can call me Miriam if you want to," she said as they walked away.

He shook his head as if to clear it. "You must forgive an old man for his foggy memory. Marianne is your name, and that is what I will call you."

Greta stood beside Toby and watched the odd couple walk away. "I have never seen my uncle smile in all the years that I have known him. Your sister has a remarkable effect on him."

"As you have had a remarkable effect on her."

"You give me too much credit. I think Christmas is the one we should thank."

"I noticed how she was acting, too. From now on, I think your uncle and the cat should stick together."

"I'm not sure Marianne will agree to that."

"She will understand. The cat belongs to you."

They returned to the van. Greta quietly explained to

Arles what had happened. "There is a hospital in Millers- burg. Do you want me to stop there?" he asked.

"Only if my uncle is feeling worse or has another at- tack."

"I'll leave it up to you, then. We should be there in thirty minutes. Hope Springs is only forty minutes from Mill- ersburg. If you don't think we should stop at the hospital, I'd like to drive straight through. I'm afraid the storm is catching up with us."

When everyone was settled, Arles pulled out and headed down the highway.

Now that she was in the home stretch of her journey, Greta found herself at a loss for words as she sat beside Toby. It was as if the companionship they shared was evap- orating the closer she got to home. Perhaps that was the way it was meant to be. Theirs was a fleeting friendship and nothing more.

As they rolled into the outskirts of Millersburg, Greta moved forward to sit beside her uncle. "How are you feel- ing?"

"Tolerable."

"We can stop if you would like."

He sneered and then looked away. "A happy family re- union awaits me. Why would I wish to delay that?"

Greta knew Arles overheard them. She caught his eye in the rearview mirror and shook her head. There was no need to stop.

Beyond Millersburg, they ran into heavy snow as they passed the leading edge of the storm. The wind drove it down the highway in white slithering snakes and began to pile it in drifts along the edges of the roadway. Heavy gusts buffeted the vehicle, forcing Arles to slow down. The forty-minute journey stretched into an hour, but fi- nally her grandfather's mailbox came into view at the side of the road.

"Turn left here," she said.

Arles braked, but the van fishtailed and skidded past the lane before he brought it back under control. "Sorry about that, folks. There must be some ice under the snow."

He managed to turn the vehicle around and safely negotiated the corner at a much slower speed. When her grandfather's house and barns came into view, Greta was both grateful and sad. She was home, but her time with Toby was done.

Arles stopped in front of the gate but left the engine running. "I'll help you get your bags out."

"I'll help her," Toby offered.

As Greta and her uncle stepped out, Marianne slipped the cat back into the pet carrier. "Goodbye, Christmas. I hope you like the farm. It's got to be better than that town."

She fastened the top closed. Her lower lip was quivering, but she bravely offered the box to Greta. "I know you'll take good care of her."

Greta folded her arms. "I was thinking that she might be happier living with you."

"Really?" Marianne's eyes brightened.

"Really. I'm afraid that our dog will chase her."

Morris shifted from one foot to the other. "He is a savage beast. The cat will be safer with you."

"Are you sure about this?" Toby asked, giving Morris a direct look.

"I shall have all my loving nieces to attend to me. Let the child have the cat. I'm going inside. It's cold out here."

Marianne put the carrier back on the seat. Then she jumped out of the vehicle and threw her arms around Morris. "Goodbye and thank you for letting me keep Christmas. I hope you get well soon. I will remember you in my prayers every night and every morning."

"Bless you, Miriam. You are a good child." He turned away, climbed the steps slowly and went into the house.

Greta dropped to her knees before Marianne ignoring the snow that covered the ground. The child threw her arms around Greta's neck and hugged her tight. "I'm going to miss you, Greta."

"I'm going to miss you, too. Take good care of Christmas for me. And remember, she isn't ugly because she has a good heart. Never believe anyone who says otherwise."

"I'll remember."

"You had better get back in the van. Smile. You will be home in a few hours."

Marianne got in and waved. "Goodbye and happy Christmas."

"Happy Christmas to you and to Christmas, too." She closed the door of the van to keep out the cold.

Toby carried Greta's bag up the porch steps, and she followed him. Now was her chance to say goodbye without an audience. He turned to face her and everything she wanted to say flew out of her mind. The only refrain in her head was something she couldn't say.

Don't go.

The snow whirled around the house, enclosing them in a cocoon of white. Toby was reluctant to leave. In two short days, she'd had a remarkable impact on him. He knew he would never forget her. "You made it home safe and sound."

"It was an interesting journey."

She didn't move toward the door. It gave him the courage to take a step closer. "I know you must think I'm a bold fellow, but I was wondering if I might write to you. Please?"

"I would like to know how your sister is doing and how Christmas is getting along."

He pushed his hands deeper into the pockets of his coat. She cared about his sister and about the cat, but did she care about him? "I hope you and your uncle can make amends."

"*Danki*. I know you and your sister will do fine."

"I should get going. The snow was getting heavier. I know Arles wants to leave."

He started to turn away, but she stopped him when she said, "I will want to know how you are getting along in Pennsylvania, too."

He smiled, happy to know she did care about him and gave her the address. He'd already made a mental note of the number on her mailbox. "I want to hear all about your schooling and how your uncle gets along with your sisters and the dog."

"I wish you could come in and meet my family."

"If I ever get back this way, I'll stay long enough to meet all of them."

"I would like that," she said softly. He couldn't be sure, but he thought she might be blushing.

"Goodbye and Merry Christmas, Greta Barkman. May God bless and keep you."

She lifted her gaze to stare into his eyes. "And you, Toby."

He wanted to kiss her more than he had ever wanted anything in his life. He took another step closer. Arles beeped the horn.

"Have a safe trip." She lifted her face ever so slightly to gaze up at him. Her lips, so close to his own, were an invitation he couldn't resist. He bent forward and covered her mouth with his own.

She pulled back in surprise, her eyes wide with shock.

He called himself every kind of fool. This wasn't how he wanted their time together to end. "I'm sorry, Greta. I didn't mean to startle you."

She pressed her fingers to her lips. "Don't be sorry."

His heart thudded against his chest. Sandwiched some-where between disappointment and hope.

I wanted one kiss to remember you by. One touch of your sweet lips to last a lifetime.

"I'm not sorry I kissed you. I'm only sorry if I fright-ened you."

"Goodbye, Toby." She picked up her bag and hurried into the house.

Arles sounded the horn again, and Toby trudged down the steps to the waiting van. He had probably given Greta a disgust of him.

Probably? She couldn't wait to get away and safely in the house. He was blessed that she hadn't set the dog on him.

What a fool he was. She would never write to him now.

As they pulled out of the farmyard, Toby looked back at the house. The snow quickly hid it from his sight. He missed her already. There was something about her pres-ence that was comforting and yet in a strange way excit-ing. Would he ever see her again? It was unlikely unless he made a point of returning to Hope Springs. Once he and Marianne were settled, could he return then? First, he had to find a job and then save enough money. How long would it take? A year? Two years? He had no way of knowing. His heart grew heavy as he realized how im-probable his plan was.

One kiss would have to be enough.

Christmas began yowling loudly and scratching at her box. Marianne opened the lid to peek in. "What's wrong?"

Christmas nudged her way out and before Marianne could stop her, she leaped over the front seat and onto Arles's shoulder. He yelped in surprise. The van swerved wildly, skidded sideways and plunged off the road.

Chapter Thirteen

Greta stood with her back against the door, her hand pressed to her chest trying to still her wildly beating heart. Why had Toby kissed her? What had he meant by it? Anything? Had he been toying with her the whole trip? Had he been bored enough to start a flirtation with her? Had her inexperience amused him?

Or, had she tempted him in some way she wasn't aware of?

Did he think she wanted his kiss, that she had low morals and didn't care about what was proper? They were little more than strangers. A good Amish woman never kissed a man she barely knew.

She raised her fingers to her lips. They still tingled from his touch.

Why didn't I kiss him back?

If only she could return to the moment and see what that would have been like. Instead, she ran away like a frightened rabbit. She would regret that for the rest of her life.

What if no one ever kisses me again?

"Where is everyone?" Morris asked. He stood in the doorway that led to the living room.

Greta pushed away from the door. She refused to believe the worst of Toby. She would remember him fondly and treasure his gesture. Her amazing journey had come to an end. A very special man had come into her life for two days and now he was gone. Reality was waiting for her. She heard footsteps coming down the stairs.

"Welcome to our home." Naomi gave Morris a tentative smile. Greta's grandfather stood behind her. He wasn't smiling. Betsy and Lizzie came in behind them. Duncan, standing at Lizzie's side, growled low in his throat. Lizzie shushed him.

"*Danki* for inviting me." Morris inclined his head slightly, but his voice was laced with sarcasm.

Naomi came forward. "I have your room ready if you would like to lie down for a while."

His shoulders slumped. "That would be nice. Traveling has been tiring." He suddenly looked as weary as he sounded.

"I understand. Please, come this way. Joseph, would you bring his bags?"

She led Morris out of the kitchen and into the living room. Instead of heading up the stairs, she turned left down a short hall and held open the door to Joseph's bedroom.

Joseph came forward and kissed Greta's cheek. "I'm glad to have my *goot* Greta with me once more. How was your trip?"

"Interesting."

"You'll have to tell us all about it." Joseph hefted a suitcase in each hand. "First, I have to give up my bed to him. Now, I'm expected to carry his bags, too. The things I do for that woman." He marched out of the kitchen.

Betsy and Lizzie raced to throw their arms around Greta. Lizzie said, "We're so glad you're home. Was it awful traveling with him?"

"Of course it was awful," Betsy said.

Greta hugged them each in turn. "It wasn't fun, but it was not awful. I had quite an adventure, but I will wait till Naomi and *Daadi* return to share everything. I would dearly love a cup of tea."

"I'll fix one for you," Betsy said, already on her way to the stove.

Greta held Lizzie's hands. "How are you?"

"I've been feeling much better. I saw the doctor yesterday and he thinks the worst is behind me."

"I'm so glad. I've been worried about you. Where is Carl?"

"He is out in the barn. We've got two sick ewes he's looking after. He should be back any moment."

Naomi and Joseph returned to the kitchen by the time the teakettle began to whistle. Joe had a deep scowl on his face. "He says the battery-operated lamp in his room is too fancy. He wants a kerosene one." He opened a cabinet door and withdrew a lamp with a tall glass chimney. "If this doesn't suit him, he can stay in the dark."

Naomi took a seat at the table. "Morris says he doesn't want anything to eat. I've got some leftover casserole from lunch that I can heat up if you are hungry, Greta."

"*Nee,* I'm fine. Only a little tired, too."

"Here's your tea," Betsy said, placing a mug on the table.

"*Danki.*" Greta sat down with a sigh. Picking up the mug, she blew on it before taking a sip. It was hot and delicious, exactly what she needed.

"Tell us the whole story," Betsy said, sliding into the seat beside Greta.

"*Ja,* tell us the whole sorry tale," Lizzie said, taking a chair on the other side.

Joseph returned and sat at the head of the table. Naomi took usual her seat at his left-hand side.

Greta smiled at her family. No words could express how wonderful it was to be with them again but she had to try. "First, I want to say how good it is to be home."

"Tell us about your trip," Betsy urged.

"You girls remember how long the bus trip was coming this way. I can assure you it is just as long on the return trip. Our van driver, Arles Hooper, met me at the bus station. There was an Amish family named Coblentz waiting for the same van. A young Amish fellow named Toby Yoder and his sister joined us at the hospital where we picked up *Onkel* Morris. Marianne, Toby's sister, had been burned in a house fire that killed their parents. Her brother is taking her to Pennsylvania to live with some family there. And then there was a cat named Christmas who joined us, but I'm getting ahead of myself. What I really need to talk to you about is what the nurse at the hospital told me about *Onkel* Morris."

Duncan dashed out from under the table and began barking. The outside door flew open with a bang. Toby staggered in with Marianne in his arms. Blood dripped down the side of his face.

Chapter Fourteen

Toby stared at the array of shocked faces around the kitchen table. The room began to spin. He fell to one knee but managed not to drop Marianne who was whimpering as she clung to him.

Greta jumped to her feet and hurried toward him. "Toby, what happened?"

"Marianne needs help. The van ran off the road."

The elderly man with Greta lifted Marianne from Toby's arms. An older woman began issuing orders. "Take her in to the sofa, Joseph. Lizzie, fetch some towels, antiseptic and bandages from the bathroom. Betsy, Greta, get this young man into the other room."

The women helped him to his feet, but he staggered when things started spinning again. Greta immediately pulled his arm around her neck and grasped him around the waist. "Lean on me."

She was much stronger than he expected and she smelled so good, but he could only rest for a moment. He tried to pull away. "Arles is still in the van. He's hurt, too."

Greta refused to let go of him. "You are in no shape to go back out into the storm."

Betsy left his side and began putting on her coat. "I'll get Carl. Where's the van?"

"Near the creek that's north of your lane. We hit a stone wall."

"I know the place. Duncan, come," she commanded. The dog followed her outside.

Relieved to know he didn't have to stagger back to the vehicle, Toby closed his eyes but the spinning sensation continued.

"Can you make it into the other room?" Greta asked.

"I'm covered with snow. I'll make a mess."

"A little water on the floor is a small concern. It's the blood dripping from your head that I'm worried about."

One of the sisters hurried back into the room. She held out a towel. Greta took it and pressed it to the side of Toby's head making him wince with pain. "*Danki,* Lizzie. Keep this tight against the cut, Toby."

He managed to hold the towel to his head and not fall as Greta led him to the doorway at the far end of the living room. Marianne was being helped out of her coat by the elderly couple. She was awake, but she still seemed dazed. She didn't protest when the woman took her bonnet and laid it on the folded coat. Toby hadn't seen her without the oversize head covering since they'd left the hospital. Their eyes met across the room. Hers widened with shock. "Toby, you're hurt!"

He stopped leaning on Greta, straightened and pointed to the towel pressed against the side of his head. "This? It's a scratch."

She pressed her lips into a tight line to stop their quivering. Toby hated to see her upset, but he was in no shape to do anything about it.

"It's a scratch that needs looking after," Greta said. She steered him to a chair. He sank gratefully into it, happy to see she had chosen one that faced away from Marianne. She didn't need to be frightened by a badly bleeding head wound even if it was only a scratch.

The woman who had handed him the towel now stood beside him with a basin of water. Greta gently sponged the area near his scalp. "It's not bad enough to need stitches. Toby, this is my sister Lizzie. Over there is my grandfather, Joseph Shetler, and his wife, Naomi."

"Nice to meet you all of you. Ouch!" He jerked away from Greta and the antiseptic she was using.

"Don't be a baby."

"Is that your way of saying you're sorry you hurt me? I would rather have a little more sympathy."

"You poor fellow. I'm so sorry. This is going to sting." She didn't sound the least bit sorry as she dabbed a cotton ball against his wound. He hissed at the burn. Was this her way of getting back at him for kissing her?

"That's the worst of it." She opened a large bandage and carefully applied it to his forehead.

The doorway down a short hall opened. Morris scowled at everyone. "What's going on?"

"There was an accident. The van skidded off the road and hit a stone wall," Toby told him.

Greta finished taping the bandage in place. She rose to her feet, looking contrite. "I'm sorry we disturbed you. We will be quieter."

"Is the little girl okay?" Morris looked around the room.

"I'm fine," Marianne said.

Toby noticed the relief in Morris's eyes. The old man had taken a liking to his sister. But why was Greta cowering in front of him?

"What about the driver?" Morris asked.

"I had to leave him in the van," Toby said.

"Betsy and Carl are seeing to him," Greta added.

Morris leaned heavily against the door frame and pressed a hand to his heart. Greta quickly crossed the room to his side. "Where are your pills? Do you need one?"

He shook his head. "I have put them on the nightstand, but I don't need one. I think I will lie down again."

"Of course." She stepped back as he closed the door.

Toby heard the front door open and started to get up, but Greta pushed him back into the chair. "Stay put. I can only deal with one patient at a time."

She and Lizzie headed into the kitchen. Marianne came to Toby's side. She had a goose egg on her forehead. "Are you sure you're okay?"

He took her hand. "I'm a little banged up, that's all. You should put some ice on that bump."

"I was just on my way to get some for her," Naomi said. "I'll bring some for you, too."

Duncan, the large black-and-white dog with tan points, came into the living room. He stopped to sniff at Toby and Marianne and then began to wag his tail.

"He likes you," Joseph said.

Marianne eyed the dog warily. "Greta said he bit her uncle."

"He did, but I don't think he liked the taste of that old buzzard. He won't do it again. You can pet him. He likes girls. Of course, he would have to since he lives in a house full of them."

Marianne stretched out her hand. Duncan licked her fingers and made her smile. Suddenly, her smile faded and she looked at Toby. "Where is Christmas?"

"I think she's still in the van." Her precious cat was responsible for the wreck. Would Arles expect Toby to pay for the damages? He had every right to. It would take a while but Toby would pay him back.

"I have to go get her," Marianne said.

Toby shook his head, but it made his dizziness worse. "You're not going out into that storm. She's fine where she is."

"She's not fine. She's scared and she's hurt. I have to go get her." Marianne dashed away from Toby and ran out of the room.

Chapter Fifteen

Greta was helping Betsy get Arles out of his coat when she saw Toby's sister dart toward the front door. "Marianne, what are you doing?"

"I have to find Christmas."

"You can't go out dressed like that!" Greta leaped to shut the door as the child tried to pull it open.

Marianne wore a white prayer *kapp* over her blond hair. The gauzy white bonnet was see-through, as was the practice in some Amish churches. It was heart-shaped in the back and sat behind the child's ears and offered no protection from the wind and snow. Greta was able to see for the first time the extent of the burns on the girl's neck and face.

Her left ear was small, deformed and still an angry red color. Part of her hair had burned away above her ear; part of it had been cut off. The puckered scars extended down her neck to vanish under the collar of her dark green dress. Marianne had suffered a great deal and Greta's heart when out to her. She glanced at her family members. Their eyes were filled with sympathy.

"Is Christmas by chance this tortoiseshell cat?" Carl asked from his place by the stove. He held a bundle in his arms. He uncovered one end and the cat's head popped out. She meowed her displeasure.

Marianne ran toward him. "Christmas, are you okay?"

Carl handed her the bundle. Christmas began purring and rubbing her head against Marianne's chin.

"I think she is happy to see you," Carl said.

"I'm happy to see her, too."

Betsy hung up Arles's coat and came to look at the cat. "My, isn't she a pretty color. Like a kitty rainbow. She looks quite handsome in her bonnet, doesn't she, Naomi?"

Naomi and Lizzie gathered around Marianne. "Very handsome. And such a sweet personality. She doesn't appear upset at all by her strange surroundings."

"She's very calm and affectionate. She hasn't even scratched at her stitches," Marianne said, concentrating on showing off her pet. She didn't seem to realize she was the center of attention, as well.

"That's because she has a calm and affectionate owner," Carl said. "Animals learn a lot from the people around them. I don't think she is any worse for wear. That's more than I can say about Mr. Hooper."

Looking contrite, Marianne turned to the driver. "I'm sorry Christmas jumped on you and made us crash. Did you get hurt?"

He held one arm folded across his chest. "The seat belt kept me from being thrown around the way you and your brother were. I surely do wish you folks would put a little more faith in them."

"God is our protection, Mr. Hooper," Naomi said.

"I know that's your belief. I respect it, but this is the first time me or anyone has been hurt while I was driving."

"I am truly sorry," Marianne said, holding Christmas closer.

Naomi examined the bump on Marianne's head. "*Gott* had a reason for stopping the car, child. Your pet was only an instrument of His plan. Here is an ice pack for that goose egg, and here's one for your brother. Come along, I want you to rest on the couch until supper is ready."

"Okay." Marianne allowed herself to be shepherded out of the kitchen.

Greta looked at Lizzie and Carl. "*Danki*. She is very self-conscious about her looks."

Lizzie slipped an arm around her husband's waist and smiled at him. "I'm used to dealing with odd-looking folks."

"Hey, who are you calling odd looking? You're the one who will resemble a pumpkin in a few months. Don't forget that."

Greta smiled at their teasing and sat down beside Mr. Hooper to examine his arm. His wrist was swollen and turning purple-blue. "What happened?"

"When the airbag deployed, it was like a hammer hitting my wrist. I hope it's not broken. My poor van's in bad shape. I'm afraid I'm not going to get those folks to Bird-in-Hand tonight. Even if I could get a tow truck to pull her out, I don't think she's drivable." He looked ready to cry.

Greta felt sorry for the man who loved his van as much as her grandfather loved his sheep. "There's no point in worrying about that tonight. Let me bandage that wrist for you. It will feel much better with some support. We will decide what's best to do in the morning."

Carl said, "There is a phone shack a half mile past the end of our lane. I will call a tow truck for you tomorrow. There's a garage on the other side of Hope Springs out by the interstate. The mechanic there has a good reputation. I'm sure he can fix your van."

"I hope so. I have Amish folks depending on me to drive them places over the holidays."

"Can't you use your cell phone to call?" Greta asked.

"It got busted in the crash. It's useless."

Naomi came into the room. "We must give thanks that this accident wasn't worse. I could use some help getting supper ready for everyone. Betsy, would you run down to the cellar and fetch up two jars of the corn you girls put up last summer? Lizzie, do you feel up to making dumplings? I've got some canned chicken I can whip into soup. Greta, when you are finished with Mr. Hooper, would you get some of my rhubarb pie filling out of the pantry? I think a couple of your wonderful hot pies will be *goot* on a cold evening like this."

"Can I make peach?" Greta asked, thinking of Marianne's preference.

Naomi smiled at her. "Make whatever you like, child. Having you home again is *wunderbarr.*"

While Naomi and the rest of the women set about preparing to feed their unexpected guests, Greta bandaged Mr. Hooper's wrist. After she was finished with him, she went to check on Toby and Marianne. Her grandfather and Carl were visiting with them. Arles followed her in, and her grandfather gave up his recliner to the *Englisch* driver, even going so far as to fetch him a pillow to prop up his arm.

Toby and Marianne were seated together on the sofa holding ice packs to their heads. Christmas lay curled in Marianne's lap looking as Amish as her owner with her head bandaged and her chin resting on her paws as if in prayer. The cat's gaze was fixed on Duncan sitting beside Carl. She gave an occasional low growl in her throat.

Greta approached Toby. "Let me take a look at that dressing. I want to make sure the bleeding has stopped."

He removed the ice pack and tipped his head so she could see. "How does it look?"

She reached to brush his hair back, but hesitated and quickly put her hand down when she saw Carl watching her. She and Toby weren't traveling in the back of the van anymore. That kind of familiarity would not be accepted by her family. She was expected to be circumspect around men. She clasped her hands together and kept her tone neutral. "It looks fine."

Toby tried to make a joke out of it. "I reckon my hard head is a blessing."

He wanted to see her soft smile, the one that warmed him all the way through. He wanted to recapture the easy camaraderie they'd shared, but Greta didn't smile at his jest. Was she angry with him? His heart sank.

She had every right to be. A modest Amish *maedel* might not kiss a fellow until they were engaged, maybe not even until their wedding day. He had cheapened their relationship with his impulsive behavior.

Surely, she didn't think he considered her a loose woman. Nothing could be further from the truth. How could he make her understand that? He glanced around at her family watching them. Finding time alone with her would be difficult if not impossible.

What if he couldn't undo this mistake? When would he learn to think before he acted?

"I praise God that it wasn't worse," Greta said.

He studied her, trying to pinpoint what was different about her. Then he realized she wasn't standing as tall. Her shoulders were bowed and her head lowered. He tried once more to make her smile. "Maybe He was trying to knock some sense into me."

It didn't work. She turned to his sister. "Let me see your bump, Marianne."

Marianne leaned closer and whispered, "Can I have my bonnet back? Your *mammi* took it away."

"It had some of Toby's blood on it and it was wet from the snow. Once it is washed and dried, you can have it back. Would you like to borrow one of my *kapps*?"

Marianne glanced around the room covertly. "*Ja,* please."

"Come upstairs with me and I'll find you one."

At least she was still being kind to his sister. He was grateful for that. Marianne handed him the cat who continued to growl low in her throat. He wasn't sure he actually wanted to be holding her if the big dog decided to accept her challenge. After the girls left the room, an awkward silence prevailed.

Toby looked at Arles trying to get comfortable in the chair. "Would you like this ice pack for your arm? I'm finished with it."

"Might as well try. It aches like nobody's business."

Joe stood up. "I'll give it to him. You sit and hang on to that cat. Are you still dizzy?"

"*Nee,* I'm fine." Toby handed over the ice pack.

Joe took it to Arles and returned to his chair. "How was your journey with my granddaughter and her uncle?"

"It was fine." He would need to start using a new word.

"Toby and your granddaughter got along like two peas in a pod, sir, but Mr. Barkman was something of a trial," Arles said.

Joe leveled a stern look at Toby. "Like two peas in a pod?"

Toby squirmed on the sofa and resisted the urge to loosen his collar. "Greta was a fine traveling companion. She took to my sister quickly and was able to entertain her. She was very worried about her uncle, though."

Arles chuckled. "Once the child had the cat, you two were left to entertain each other in the back."

Joe's eyes narrowed. "Exactly what type of entertainment did my granddaughter supply?"

Chapter Sixteen

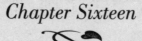

Had the temperature of the room suddenly gone up?

Toby cleared his throat while he tried to think of something that wouldn't offend Greta's grandfather. "Entertainment? We did some cross-stitch. It's something I've been meaning to take up again. She's a good teacher."

Toby thought Carl laughed, but he turned it into a cough so Toby couldn't be sure. Joe glared at him.

The ensuing awkward silence lasted until the girls returned. Marianne wore a black *kapp* instead of her usual white one. It was a little too big, but he knew she was more comfortable with her scars covered. She sat down and took the cat from him. He brushed his sweaty palms on his pant legs.

Greta glanced from his face to her grandfather's stern one. She arched an eyebrow at Toby. He gave her a weak smile. "I was telling your grandfather about our cross-stitching lesson."

She looked perplexed. "I'm going to go help in the kitchen." She pointed in that direction.

"A good idea," her grandfather said. "I may have more questions for Toby."

Once she was out of the room, Toby went on the offensive to forestall any more inquiries from Joe or comments from Arles. "Greta told us that this is a sheep farm. How many sheep do you have, Joe?"

Joe looked at Carl. "What was our last count?"

"One hundred and eighty-five."

"How many baby lambs?" Marianne asked. Toby was surprised that she entered the conversation. She was normally reserved around people she didn't know. He was tempted to hug her.

"Lambs? None. We won't have lambs until spring," Joe said. "All we have now are pregnant mothers and four fat, lazy rams."

"What happened to your cat?" Carl asked. His dog sat beside him, but the animal's gaze was fixed on the doorway to Morris's room.

Marianne stroked the cat's back. "She got caught in the engine of Mr. Hooper's van. She's really Greta's cat, but Greta gave her to me before we left. She was afraid your dog wouldn't like her."

Carl reached down to pet Duncan's head. "Greta is right about that. Duncan likes to chase cats, but I think he will behave if I tell him he must. Should we introduce them and see how it goes?"

Marianne clutched Christmas to her chest. "Not tonight. Christmas is grumpy. She might hurt your dog."

There was a second of silence, then everyone laughed. Marianne scowled at the men guffawing around her.

Joe wiped a tear from his eye. "Poor Duncan, think what a blow that would be to his self-respect. I'd almost like to see it. I'm sure the cat could give him what for."

To Toby's surprise, Marianne began laughing, too. She grinned at Carl. "She might. She's a scrapper."

Toby settled back on the couch. It was worth a bump on the head and much more to hear his sister laugh again. Who would have thought a scrawny stray cat could be such good medicine.

"In that case we had better make sure Duncan leaves her alone," Carl said with a wide grin.

After that, the men discussed the weather and what it might mean for the price of food and fuel if the storm lived up to predictions. When the conversation lagged, Toby remembered his first chat with Greta about sheep. "Do you have to worry about sheep in weather like this or do you keep them in the barn over the winter?"

Joe said, "Can't really keep sheep inside barns for any length of time unless you have very good ventilation. They're prone to respiratory infections. We graze them in open pastures during the winter. We set aside several tracks of land during the fall and let the grass reach eight to ten inches in height. Even with a good snowfall on that, it won't go completely flat. They can paw their way down to it."

"We have round bales of hay available for them, too," Carl added.

"Will they graze even in the storm like this?" Toby asked.

"Sheep are ruminants. They tend to fill up prior to a storm. Then they can wait it out in a sheltered spot and just chew their cud. They can go up to two days without eating, and it will not cause them harm."

"What about water?"

"If they can't get to water, they eat the snow. Sometimes they would rather eat the snow than go to fresh water."

Toby noticed Greta was mixing dough on the counter near the doorway and listening to the conversation. She kept glancing in his direction. Her grandfather was an eagle-eyed fellow. He noticed, too. "What else did you and Greta talk about?"

What had they talked about? Toby remembered the feeling of comfortable companionship more than he remembered individual conversations. He glanced at her. "We talked a little about her schooling."

Her eyes widened and she gave a quick shake of her head.

He winced inwardly. Wrong topic.

Joe's eyes narrowed. "What about her schooling?"

"Just that she liked school…and she hoped that my sister would like school in Pennsylvania…and that her sisters all enjoyed their schooling." Toby stumbled to a halt knowing he sounded like a fool.

Carl had his fingers pressed against his mouth but his eyes were crinkled with amusement. "Did she mention that her sister Clara had hoped to become a schoolteacher but decided to marry instead?"

Toby started to nod but changed it to a shake. "*Nee,* I don't think she did."

Greta rolled her eyes at him and went back to kneading her dough.

"And what is it that you do, Toby?" Carl asked.

"I'm a wood-carver by trade, but I was working in one of the RV factories in Fort Wayne until recently."

Arles lost his frown of pain and sat up with interest. "Which one?"

Toby gave him the name and it opened a floodgate of questions from the driver about various models, gas mileage and upgrades. It seemed that he was eager to explore more of the country and thought an RV might be perfect for him since he enjoyed driving.

Toby was able to relax a little as he answered Arles's questions, but he had the feeling that Joe would keep an eye on him during their stay. His chance to find time alone with Greta was diminishing.

It was some time later that Naomi came to the doorway and announced dinner. Duncan left his place by Carl's chair and stood at the back door. Carl let him out. Marianne fixed a place on the couch with a pillow and a crocheted throw. She put Christmas inside the makeshift nest, and the cat seemed content to stay put.

Supper turned out to be a delicious and generous spread

with chicken and dumplings, golden yellow corn, green beans, homemade bread with blueberry jam and two peach pies for dessert. Toby hadn't eaten so well in weeks. He was glad to see Marianne did justice to her plate, but it wasn't long before her eyelids began to droop. He had to remember this was only her second day out of the hospital. Greta had been watching his sister, too.

He caught her eye and tipped his head toward the stairs. She nodded. He smiled his thanks. She quickly looked around to see who might be watching them. She didn't smile back. His heart sank. Had he lost her friendship for good?

Greta was glad to get away from the table. It was hard to have Toby so close and not speak to him. She rose from her place and touched Marianne's shoulder. "Let's get you and Christmas off to bed. It has been a very long day."

"Can Christmas sleep with me?"

"Of course."

"Will the dog bother her during the night?"

Joe said, "Duncan normally sleeps on the back porch so he can go out and keep an eye on the farm at night. Your cat will be safe inside."

Naomi said, "Joe, why don't you fetch one of the little beds from the attic for Marianne."

"I was just going to do that." He pushed away from the table with a wink for his wife.

Marianne collected Christmas from the sofa and followed Greta upstairs. In Greta's room, she stifled a wide yawn. "We need to feed Christmas. She must be hungry by now."

"I have some of the food the vet gave us right here." Greta handed a packet to Marianne who made a small pile of the kibble on the floor. Christmas made short work of her meal.

Joseph brought the bed into Greta's room and Naomi made it up for the girl. After they left, Greta fixed a make-shift litter box from an old cake pan and filled a bowl with water for the cat. She immediately came to get a drink.

Marianne stroked her pet lovingly. "She likes it here. Everyone is friendly, and they didn't make fun of the way she looks."

"My family loves animals. We take care of sick and hurt ones all the time. Why, you should see this house during lambing season. We have bottle lambs everywhere. I've even seen *Daadi* Joe holding two in his lap and feeding them in his recliner."

Looking up, Marianne's eyes grew sad. "I think she wants to stay here."

Greta shook her head. "I think she only wants to visit for a little while. Until the storm is over. Then, she has a new family to meet who will love her and not make fun of her."

"I hope so."

"I know so. If she is ever unhappy, all she has to do is think about me and my family and how much we like her."

Marianne smiled. "I will. I mean, she will."

Greta stayed where she was to make sure Marianne fell asleep. At least that's what she told herself.

The truth was that she was hiding out. It was better than going downstairs to face Toby for the evening. Bandaging his head was one thing. Making small talk was another. His kiss was constantly on her mind. Everyone was sure to see how distracted she was.

Why had he done it? Did he regret it? Would he try to repeat it?

If he did, what would she do? Her thoughts ran around like spring lambs in the pasture, leaping this way and that without settling on a solution to her problem.

How could she pretend the kiss hadn't happened?

It wasn't long before her sister Betsy came upstairs. "I

think we have everyone settled. Toby chose to sleep on the sofa. Arles elected to sleep in Joseph's recliner with his arm resting on a stack of pillows. Naomi and *Daadi* have taken over my room so that Morris wouldn't have to climb the stairs. Carl and Lizzie are in their usual bedroom down at the end of the hall. It looks like you're stuck with me." She began getting ready for bed. She took off her *kapp* and let down her hair.

Greta did the same. "I don't mind."

"I knew you wouldn't. How is Marianne?"

"Sleeping." Christmas was curled up on the pillow beside her head.

"Have you looked out the window? It's still snowing heavily. I wonder how long our guests will be stuck here? I hope they stay until Christmas. Wouldn't that be fun?"

Five more days? Greta didn't think she could take it. "I'm sure it will blow itself out tonight. Marianne and her brother have family anxious to spend Christmas with them. How is *Onkel* Morris?"

"I don't know. He hasn't poked his head out."

"Do you think we should check on him?"

"Ugh, not me. I don't want to get my head chewed off. You never did tell us about your trip. Was it awful?"

Nee, it was wonderful.

She could hardly admit that without explaining why. Instead, she said, "I'm glad it's over. I wanted to tell everyone together, but I will tell you now. The nurse at the hospital told me *Onkel* Morris isn't going to get better. He may only have a few months left to live."

Betsy sank onto the foot of the bed. "Are you serious?"

"I am."

Betsy gripped her hands together and was silent for a long time. Finally, she looked up. "Does he know?"

"*Ja.*"

"Has it…has it changed him?"

"Not that I can tell."

"I feel bad now for imagining that I could sic Duncan on him if he made me angry. It was very unchristian of me, but I did enjoy the thought."

Greta's chuckled. "I know what you mean."

"You and *Daadi* were right. *Onkel* Morris has found a way to ruin our Christmas."

Greta crossed the room to give her sister a hug. "We must not let that happen. We will have a wonderful Christmas, and together we can show him all that he has missed. Who knows, maybe the Lord will use the love in this house to change our uncle's heart before it is too late."

"Well, He has been known to work miracles."

"Indeed He has." Greta began to giggle, and Betsy joined in, both holding their hands over their mouth so they wouldn't wake the sleeping child.

They were still giggling when they blew out the lamp and crawled under the covers. Even though she was dead tired, Greta found it hard to sleep knowing that Toby was just downstairs. When she got out of the van that afternoon, she never expected to see him again, and yet God had sent him right back to her. What did it mean?

Why give them another day together? Wasn't a clean break the best? Oh, she wanted to spend more time with him, but even if he stayed another day, he was still going to leave. Her heart ached at the thought. She punched her pillow into shape.

She would recover from this loss. The strange feeling that made her giddy when she was near him would fade with time and distance. She was too practical a person to dream about a man who was far away. Wasn't she?

Closing her eyes, she concentrated on not thinking. It didn't help. In desperation, she began counting sheep. At three hundred, she stopped that futile exercise, too.

Rolling over carefully so as not to disturb Betsy, Greta

saw Christmas had made herself at home on the window ledge. She sat peering intently out into the night. Greta listened, but heard nothing except the wind and the hiss of snow against the window panes. What was the cat looking at?

Chapter Seventeen

Rising, Greta moved to the window, crossing her arms to ward off the chill. She pulled back the simple white curtain and tried to look out. All she could see was the swirling darkness. No hint of light from the moon or stars penetrated the blizzard raging outside. Even their *Englisch* neighbor's yard light, normally visible from Greta's window, was hidden from view. The howling wind continued unabated. Toby and his sister wouldn't be leaving in the morning.

The cat licked her paw and looked at Greta. She ran a hand down the animal's sleek back. The cat arched into her hand and purred.

"I'm sure you're happy to have a warm place to sleep and all the food you can eat, but you will have that in Pennsylvania, too. Why make everyone stay here? He kissed me. What am I supposed to say to him tomorrow? How shall I act?"

Christmas yawned, her pink tongue curling back on her white teeth. She lay down and began to lick her paws.

"I see you have no answer for me. Why am I surprised?" Greta leaned her forehead on the cold glass. "I have no answer for me, either."

Tomorrow would come soon enough.

Somehow, she would find a way to get through it.

In spite of her sleepless night, Greta was the first one up

in the morning. She crept into the kitchen expecting to find it empty, but Toby stood with his back to her as he gazed out the window over the sink. She paused in the doorway. She didn't know what to say. She didn't know how to act. She took a step back, intending to return upstairs.

He turned around, but the sweet smile that she expected was missing from his face. "Good morning."

She stiffened her back and lifted her chin. "Good morning. I was about to put on some coffee."

"That sounds good. It's still snowing. I don't think we are going anywhere today."

He looked wonderful in the soft morning light. His hair was rumpled. There was stubble on his cheeks and his clothes were the same ones that he had been wearing yesterday. She had never seen a better looking man.

"How's your head?" she asked, trying hard to conceal how much she cared.

He touched the bandage. "Sore."

"I'm not surprised." She took the coffeepot from the back of the stove and carried it to the sink, forcing him to step aside. He was so close that her nerve endings tingled with awareness. She concentrated on keeping her hands steady.

"Greta, about yesterday…" His voice trailed away.

She turned toward him clasping the coffeepot to her chest as if it could shield her from heartache. "What about it?"

"I was out of line."

He was going to say he was sorry again. She didn't want to hear that. "I'd rather not talk about it."

"Please know that it was never my intention to hurt you."

She turned to the sink and began filling the pot with water. "It was just a kiss, Toby. Don't tell me you've never kissed a girl before." She would die before she told him it had been her first. Very likely her last.

"I have kissed one or two girls, but it didn't mean anything."

She smiled so brightly that her cheeks hurt and turned to face him. "Well, there you go. We can agree that it didn't mean anything. Now, can we talk about something else?"

All night he had rehearsed this conversation in his mind instead of sleeping. He wanted to know how she felt about his impulsive but heartfelt act. He had his answer. Although it wasn't the one he wanted.

The kiss had meant a great deal to him, but clearly, it hadn't meant anything to her. She moved about the kitchen fixing coffee and getting eggs out of the refrigerator, stepping around him as if he were nothing more than an obstacle in her path, not someone she had grown fond of the way he had grown fond of her. At least she wasn't angry. That was something.

"I'll get out of your hair," he said, moving toward the living room.

"I'll call you when breakfast is ready," she said as she cracked eggs into a bowl.

She sounded so cold, so distant. He wanted to say something that would restore the closeness and the friendship that they had shared, but he feared he had ruined that forever.

He walked out of the room. At the door, he paused and looked back. She stood with her arms braced on the countertop and her head down as if the weight of the world were crushing her. He heard a muffled sniff and it cut him to the quick.

He was back at her side before the thought even formed in his mind. It took every ounce of willpower he possessed not to gather her in his arms. "Don't cry, Greta.

I'm sorry. It was foolish of me. I knew that I would never see you again, and I couldn't bear that. I meant no disrespect, although I'm sure you didn't see it that way. Please forgive me."

She straightened and scrubbed her cheeks with her palms. "There's nothing to forgive."

"I might believe that if you weren't crying. The last thing I want to lose is your friendship."

"We were friends, weren't we?" She asked in a small and timid voice.

"We *are* friends," he said firmly. "If I ever have to journey in the back of a van for two days again, I would choose you to accompany me over anyone else in the world."

She gave him a watery smile. "It was better than riding the bus."

"I'll take your word for that. Am I forgiven for my lapse of good sense? I don't think I could stand it if I knew you were still angry with me."

"I'm not angry with you."

"*Danki.* I will mind my manners from here on out." He would, no matter what it cost him. Because even now, with her wiping away tears, he still wanted to kiss her. He didn't understand this hopeless attraction to her, but he wanted her friendship. And he wanted to see her happy more than he wanted another kiss.

She sniffed again. "How do you like your eggs?"

"Over hard, break the yolks."

"I think I can manage that. Can I ask a favor?"

"Anything," he said and he meant it.

"Would you check on my uncle for me?"

"I will, and I will be as quiet as a mouse."

After Toby left the kitchen, Greta turned to the sink and splashed water on her face to erase any evidence of her tears. She scrubbed as hard as she dared. What a fool she was. She wasn't angry at Toby. She was angry at herself for making a mountain out of a molehill.

These crazy feelings that tangled her up when he was near were a mess of her own making. She had been lonely, frightened and insecure from the moment she faced her uncle again. Toby's kindness had been a balm to her wounded spirit. His friendliness was a stark contrast to her uncle's animosity. She made her relationship with Toby into more than it really was. She craved his calm gentleness and somehow she communicated that need in a way he had misinterpreted. He wasn't to blame. She would simply have to control those emotions. Now that she was home and surrounded by her family, she wouldn't need him to soothe her battered mental state.

After using a kitchen towel to blot her face, she drew a deep breath and resolved to be something other than a weeping basket case when he spoke to her. She set about fixing breakfast with a vengeance.

"So you let him kiss you. A fellow will not buy the cow if he can get the milk for free." Morris came out of the pantry just off the kitchen.

Mortified, she stared at her uncle in shock. "You were eavesdropping on us!"

He held out an orange box. "I was looking for some baking soda. I have indigestion. I couldn't help overhearing what you said. The door was ajar."

She turned away in disgust. "I don't suppose you thought of letting us know you were there."

"I did think of it."

He moved to the sink, poured a glass of water and mixed a spoonful of baking soda into the liquid. He turned around and sipped the drink slowly. Greta got on with her work and began mixing dough for biscuits.

"You know he was simply bored and using you to pass the time on our trip, don't you?"

"I don't know anything of the sort." She tried to sound defiant, but she only sounded defensive and insecure. Hadn't that very thought crossed her mind only moments after Toby kissed her?

"My poor Greta, you never were the brightest one in the bunch. Greta the mouse, always trying to scurry out of my sight."

She sucked in a breath that ended in a sob. "You heard him just now. He apologized for his action. We're friends, that's all."

"*Ja,* he is a friendly fellow. This storm will keep him here for a few more days. I imagine he will make a pass at Betsy next. She's younger and so much prettier."

Greta bit her lip. Betsy was prettier. Would Toby start paying attention to her?

No, she didn't believe that. Yet her uncle had put the idea in her head and it was hard to make it leave. "You're wrong about Toby. He's a kind man."

"And you are a weak woman. I pity you. I do."

Toby came back into the kitchen. "Your uncle is not in his room or in the bathroom. Oh, there you are, sir. How are you feeling this morning?"

Morris set his empty glass on the counter and smiled at Greta. "I'm actually feeling much better. I'm glad we had this little talk. It reminds me of old times. You remember how I like my eggs and oatmeal, don't you?"

"*Ja, Onkel.* I remember." He would sometimes throw it at her if she got it wrong. Greta swallowed hard against the bitterness rising from her stomach.

"I wasn't looking forward to coming here, but I believe I may enjoy my Christmas among the sheep." He chuckled at his own joke and left the room.

Toby moved to Greta's side. "You look upset. Is something wrong?"

She shook her head. He could never understand. "Nothing's wrong. Things are the same as they always were."

"*Nee,* you've changed since you got home."

She started laughing. "I haven't changed. This is the real me. I'm not the person you thought you knew. I'm Greta the mouse."

Chapter Eighteen

Something was definitely wrong.

Toby took a step back. He didn't care for the look of hopelessness on Greta's face or the glimmer of tears in her eyes in spite of her harsh laughter. "Greta, look at me."

She wouldn't. "Please go away, Toby. I have work to do."

"What did he say that upset you?"

"What does it matter? He says and he does whatever he wants. He isn't happy until everyone around him is unhappy. He has a knack for it and he'll never change. I just have to endure."

"And what do you have a knack for, Greta Barkman?" Toby demanded.

That caught her attention. She glanced at him and looked away. "Nothing."

"Well, you're a poor liar. So what do you have a knack for?"

"Cooking, cleaning, tending the garden, nursing sick sheep."

He crossed his arms and leaned back slightly. "Now we're getting somewhere. What else do you have a knack for, Greta Barkman?"

"Nothing, I told you that."

"So helping my sister was nothing special. Helping me talk about my grief was nothing special. Do you really not see your God-given gift? I don't believe it, because you told me yourself that you wanted to go on to school so that you could help abused women."

"It's a foolish dream. I don't know why I ever thought of it."

He stepped forward and laid a hand on her shoulder. She flinched but didn't pull away. "Because you want to help people, Greta. You have a knack for it. If a woman you want to help had been in this kitchen this morning, what would you say to her?"

"I don't know."

"Again, I will mention you are not a good liar. You know exactly what you would tell her. You would tell her to keep her mouth shut and never mention to anyone the way she was treated."

She looked up aghast. "I would never say that."

He nodded and folded his arms again. "Now I hear the ring of truth in your words. If you wouldn't tell her that, what would you tell her?"

"I would tell her to find a heavy cast-iron skillet and bang that ugly old man over the head with it."

"Okay, that is not what I expected."

The tiniest smile tugged at the corner of her lips. "I wouldn't say that, either. Nor would I ever do it. I would tell her to remember that she is a worthwhile person, not a worthless person."

He patted his chest in relief. "*Goot,* I like that much better. What else?"

She stood a little straighter. The hopelessness left her eyes. "I would tell her that God does not make junk. She is not junk. I would tell her God's love is all encompassing and no matter what our lives bring, God's love for us never wavers."

"She has to believe that in her heart or nothing will change."

Greta closed her eyes. "She has to believe that none of

it is her fault. She has to believe she deserves goodness in her life."

Toby placed a finger under her chin and lifted her face so that she had to look at him. "And do you believe that?"

Greta gazed into Toby's compassionate eyes and wondered if he had any idea how much comfort his words brought her. "I want to believe. I want to, but it's hard to change the way I have thought for so long."

"I think I understand. So what will you do about it? Do you have a plan?"

"I will pray."

"We pray for a good harvest, but we still have to hoe the ground and plant the seeds. You can't scatter them willy-nilly and expect a good crop. It takes careful planning and a family working together to gather in enough for all. You don't need to do this alone."

"You are right. I will have a meeting with my family today and we will come up with a plan. My uncle cannot revert to his old ways in this house. My family deserves goodness. *Danki,* for pointing out the obvious to me."

"It's something I have a knack for."

She bit the corner of her lip. "He was in the pantry. He overheard our conversation. He knows you kissed me."

"And you don't think he will keep that information to himself?"

"Only if it suits him. If he can use it against me somehow, he will."

"Then I am doubly sorry I gave him ammunition, but I'm still not sorry that I kissed you."

"You kissed my sister!"

Greta spun around to see Betsy in the doorway with an openmouthed look of delight on her face. Duncan stood at her side wagging his tail. Greta closed her eyes and groaned. "We have to stop having these conversations in the kitchen where everyone and their dog can overhear us."

Betsy pulled out a chair and took a seat at the table. She propped her elbows on the table and put her chin in her hands. "Duncan can keep a secret. So can I."

"There is no such thing as a secret in this house." Greta added a spoonful of shortening to the flour in her bowl.

Betsy grinned. "It's true that most of them don't stay a secret for long."

Toby took a seat across from Betsy. "I hope I can depend on you to keep this one. I don't want your sister to be embarrassed."

She laid a finger alongside her cheek and tapped it. "I'll think about it."

Greta saw the look of admiration in Betsy's eyes. From where she was standing, she couldn't see Toby's face. Was he giving her one of his heart-fluttering smiles? Did he find her attractive?

Of course he did. Betsy was as cute as a bug's ear and could be utterly charming when she put her mind to it. Much more charming than Greta knew how to be.

It was hard not to give weight to Morris's words when they were exactly what Greta feared. That Toby, kindhearted, easy-going Toby, would be himself no matter which sister he was with, that their relationship really hadn't been anything special.

Greta turned away from the pair. "While you are thinking, set the table and then bring up some more blueberry jam from the cellar. We're almost out."

Toby came to stand close beside Greta. "Breakfast can wait. I think now would be a good time to have your family meeting before Arles and Marianne are awake and Morris comes out of his room again."

She set her baking aside. She shouldn't put it off. "Betsy,

ask Lizzie and Carl to come to the quilting room upstairs. I'll get *Daadi* and Naomi."

"Why are we having a family meeting?"

Greta clasped her hands together and stared at her white knuckles. "Because *Onkel* Morris is up to his old ways."

Betsy jumped up and threw her arms around Greta. "We'll put a stop to it. Somehow."

Greta returned her sister's hug. "We will. We have to. It's our first happy Christmas together since we were little girls. We won't let him ruin it."

Fifteen minutes later, all of Greta's family sat assembled around the quilting frame that had been set up in a room with a long line of south-facing windows. Toby stood near the door to keep an eye down the hall. Greta shared the information with everyone about Morris's condition and waited for them to come to grips with it.

Lizzie smoothed the soft fabric of the quilt top with her hands. "So when Morris leaves, it won't be to go back to Indiana."

Greta sighed. "*Nee.* He will travel down the road to our Amish cemetery on Adrian Lapp's land and be laid to rest there."

Lizzie rubbed her fingers over her forehead. "It's hard to accept, isn't it? I know we all have to die, it's part of life, but knowing his end is near changes things somehow."

"I thought so, too, but he has not changed. It took him less than ten minutes to have me feeling worthless and cowering this morning. We have to be prepared for his abuse. I'm not sure if he will ever change, but if we hold each other up and refuse to allow him to hurt us, we will gain the upper hand. Perhaps then he will see that we are not his pawns."

"I'm not going to let him make me feel worthless," Lizzie declared.

"Nor am I," Betsy said.

Their grandfather, who had been quiet until this point, said, "You girls have brought light and life into this house. I am forever grateful to God for your presence. Nothing Morris can say or do will change that."

Naomi crossed her arms over her chest. "Let him try to be mean to one of you while I am listening. He may very well find himself wearing a cast-iron hat."

"Now, Naomi, you know that isn't right," their grandfather chided.

"I know, and I'm sorry for the unchristian thought, but it hurts my heart to think of him putting down my new granddaughters."

Greta met Toby's eyes and smiled. "Now do you see where I get it?"

He nodded. "You women truly make me want to mind my manners."

"And well you should," Joe said with a stern look.

"Greta, how do you suggest that we treat him?" Lizzie asked.

"The first thing is to make him aware of what he is doing. The next thing is to let him know that we will no longer tolerate that type of behavior."

Lizzie rubbed her hands up and down her arms. "That is easier said than done."

"I think we should involve the bishop." Greta waited for everyone's reaction.

Joe and Naomi shared a speaking look. Naomi said, "Bishop Zook is a good man, but Morris is not one of his flock. I'm not sure he will want to step in."

"We must kill *Onkel* Morris with kindness," Betsy said.

"What do you mean?" Lizzie asked, her face frozen with shock.

"Not literally kill him. That was a bad choice of words on my part. I mean, we want a happy and joyous Christmas season, don't we? That is exactly what we should have.

We will do all the things we have talked about. We'll bake oodles of cookies and yummy things."

"We can have a Christmas singing here if the weather cooperates." Lizzie's eyes brightened with excitement.

"Ja." Betsy rushed on. "We can make little presents for each other and put them on our plates Christmas morning, even his plate. We'll sing Christmas hymns together and *Daadi* can read the Christmas story from the Bible. We will welcome the Christ child with grateful, joyful hearts. If Morris says or does anything that takes away from the Christmas spirit in our house, we will ignore it. Forgive him and ignore it. This is our home."

"She might be right," Greta acknowledged. "Perhaps we can make Morris see what Christmas should be in a loving family."

Naomi nodded slowly. "Maybe it will change his heart and open him to God's grace."

Leaning forward eagerly, Betsy rubbed her hands together. "Where shall we start?"

Chapter Nineteen

"We start with breakfast. I'm hungry," Joe said, making Toby and the women laugh.

Greta met Toby's gaze. He saw a new determination in her eyes. She nodded. "We start with breakfast."

The Barkman sisters, working in happy concert, were a sight to behold. There was good-natured teasing, laughter and smiling faces all around. Watching from the safety of the living room, Toby leaned toward Carl. "Are they always like this?"

"Always," Joe answered for him. "I haven't had a minute's peace since they arrived."

"They are kind of loud," Arles said, struggling to get into a more comfortable position in the chair.

Joe rose and touched Arles on the shoulder. "I can put a cot for you up in the quilting room. I think you'll be more comfortable there and it will be much quieter."

"I'm willing to try anything. I didn't get much sleep last night."

"Then come along. We'll save you something to eat when you've had more rest."

Arles rose with his arm clutched to his chest. "Thank you, sir, you folks have been mighty nice to me."

As the two men went upstairs, Toby couldn't contain his amusement. "He didn't get any sleep? It was like lying beside a chain saw all night."

"I heard it up in my room. I wasn't sure if it was him or you."

"I hope it wasn't me."

"I'll let you know tomorrow. Our bedroom is beside the quilting room."

An outburst of laughter turned Toby's attention to the kitchen. He stared at the sisters in wonder. "It's hard to imagine that they were abused for years."

Carl nodded. "I know what you mean. God saw to it that they had each other. I know that helped Lizzie. I'm sure it helped the others, too. Clara is the quiet one. She normally keeps them in line, but now she has little ones of her own to ride herd on. I hope you get to meet her."

"So do I." Toby was growing fond of this family. Fonder still of Greta. He had watched her struggle against her uncle's demeaning treatment and emerge stronger.

He heard footsteps on the stairs and saw his sister come down. She had the cat in her arms. Duncan, who had been lying beside Carl's chair, sat up and eyed the newcomers. His feathery tail wagged slowly.

Carl put a hand on his dog's head. "Stay. Be easy. Marianne, is Christmas grumpy this morning?"

The girl stopped in front of Carl. "She feels fine."

"Do you want to introduce these two?"

Toby wasn't sure, but he trusted Carl to know his own dog. Marianne looked at her pet. "Okay."

"*Goot.* Bring her to me." Carl held out his hands.

"Be nice, Christmas," Marianne instructed as she handed the cat over.

Christmas stayed still, but her fur stood on end as she growled. Duncan inched closer to sniff her. Quick as a flash, Christmas smacked his snout twice. The hollow sound echoed loudly in the room. Duncan drew back, shook his head, sneezed and then lay down, looking away as if he didn't care she was on his owner's lap.

"Christmas, that wasn't nice." Marianne lifted her from Carl's lap and carried her to the couch.

Carl rubbed his dog behind one ear and checked his nose. "She didn't use her claws. At least you know she isn't a pushover. You had better leave her be."

Greta came into the room. Her back was ramrod straight. "Breakfast is ready. Please come and eat. I'll get *Onkel* Morris."

"I'll get him," Marianne said, passing the cat to Toby. She hopped off the sofa and rushed to his door. She knocked once and pushed it open. "Breakfast. Better come and get it before we throw it out. How are you this morning? Christmas thumped Duncan on the nose and he didn't bite her."

Morris emerged and patted Marianne on the head. "Did she? Well, she is a very good cat, then."

"*Ja,* I think so, too."

Joe came down the stairs. "*Guder mariye,* Morris. I hope you slept well."

Betsy and Lizzie leaned out the kitchen door. "Good morning, *Onkel,*" they said together.

He stared at them, a puzzled and distrustful expression on his face. *"Guder mariye."*

"We have oatmeal just the way you like it," Betsy said.

"And Greta made soft-boiled eggs for you, too. We know you like them."

"We'll see about that," he grumbled, but he walked into the kitchen.

Everyone took their seats. Joe sat at the head of the table. His wife sat on his left-hand side with the girls ranging down the table length by age. Carl sat at Joe's right with Toby beside him. Morris chose to sit at the foot.

Joe bowed his head and everyone prayed silently until Joe raised his head, signaling the end of his prayers. "Pass the bacon, Naomi. It sure smells *goot.*"

Morris folded his arms over his chest. "My doctor says I can't have bacon anymore. It's cruel to make me sit here and smell it while all of you enjoy it."

Naomi passed the platter to her husband. "The bacon is cooked and can't be uncooked. If you don't want to smell it, you may go back to your room."

Morris's scowl deepened, but he didn't say anything else. He added salt and pepper to his eggs, took a bite and tossed down his fork. "These eggs aren't the way I like them."

Greta leaned forward so she could see him. "We don't have more. If you don't like them, feed them to the dog. He isn't picky."

"Are you implying that I'm picky?"

"Not at all, *Onkel*. I merely said the dog isn't."

Marianne pushed her plate toward him. "You can have mine. I'm not that hungry."

"Keep your breakfast, child. I'll choke these down before I make that hound happy."

Marianne tipped her head as she regarded him. "Did you get up on the wrong side of the bed? You sure sound grumpy."

"You are impertinent. Children should be seen and not heard."

Toby watched his sister's happy expression fade and he knew a moment of intense resentment before he sent up a silent prayer asking forgiveness for the thought. Morris knew how to squash the happiness and kindness of those around him. He was more in need of prayers than anyone else at this table. Toby glanced across the table at Greta. She cast him a sympathetic look and then whispered something to Naomi.

Joe laid his fork and knife down, folded his hands and narrowed his eyes at Morris. "This is my house. I decide when someone eating at my table needs to be corrected."

Morris locked eyes with him for a long moment. Toby sensed the tense battle of wills taking place. Morris gave in first and continued eating. After a minute, Joe resumed eating, too.

Naomi smiled at her husband and winked. Toby had to take a sip of coffee to keep from laughing. She rubbed her hands together. "Today, we can start on our Christmas preparations."

"What kind of preparations?" There was a glimmer of interest in Marianne's eyes.

"We have so much to get done that I hardly know where to start," Naomi declared. "We have a ton of baking to get done. We will need at least ten dozen cookies. Several pounds of fudge and divinity."

"Don't forget the pies," Greta said quickly.

"*Nee,* I must not forget the pies. Blueberry, peach, cherry, rhubarb, pumpkin. Am I forgetting any? Morris, what is your favorite kind of pie?"

"Shoofly," he said hesitantly.

Naomi nodded to him. "Then you shall have it, for we want you to feel that you are part of our family now."

"Of course you do." His sarcasm wasn't lost on anyone.

The sisters exchanged glances. Betsy said, "It's true, *Onkel* Morris. We want you to feel at home here."

"I'll believe that when I see it."

"We do. It's Christmas, after all," Lizzie added.

"Marianne, what things does your family do to get ready for Christmas?" Greta asked. Toby noticed she didn't try to convince Morris that he was wanted.

His sister had regained some of her animation. "We always have a program at school. I won't be in it this year, but I will watch my cousins put on a play and sing Christmas songs."

"Our school has a program, too," Naomi said. "Hearing

the children singing is the highlight of the evening for me. What other things do you do to get ready for Christmas?"

"*Mamm* and I would go shopping. She let me pick out a present for Toby last year."

He smiled at her. "They were a fine pair of leather gloves, and they kept my fingers warm and cozy. Don't forget the pine boughs that *Daed* would bring in for *Mamm*."

Marianne smiled at the memory. "She would put them on the mantel and in the window with a candle."

"What a *goot* idea," Naomi said. "I love the smell of cedar and pine in the house. Joseph, you must bring some in for me."

He looked at her over his cup of coffee. "Can I finish my breakfast first?"

She laughed. "*Ja,* you can wait until the blizzard is over, too."

"That's mighty kind of you. I believe I will."

Morris leaned back in his chair and folded his arms. "My church does not approve of such frivolity. We would never be allowed to decorate our homes in such an *Englisch* fashion."

Joe's smile faded. "I know that your church adheres strongly to the old ways, and I respect that, but here in Hope Springs we are a little less strict."

"Don't expect me to embrace your church's Ordnung." Morris pushed back his chair and rose to his feet.

"We wouldn't dream of it," Naomi said. "I hope you understand that we *do* embrace it."

Morris left the room. Joe and Carl briefly discussed the chores and preparations that needed to be done that day while Naomi and the sisters quickly cleaned up the kitchen. Marianne went upstairs to feed Christmas and to give her the antibiotic the vet had prescribed.

Carl looked at Joe. "We can't put it off much longer.

Since the storm is keeping us inside, we might as well get started on your taxes."

Joe groaned. "'Render therefore unto Caesar the things which be Caesar's, and unto God the things which be God's.'"

"First, you need to give unto Carl all your bills and receipts so I can see that you don't overpay. Or do you want to use a tax man this year?"

He slapped Carl on the shoulder. "I trust you to do a fair job."

"I'm cheaper, too. That doesn't hurt. I think you like to see me pull my hair out. Do you have receipts for the medicine and the vet bills from last summer's wild dog attack on our lambs?"

"Somewhere."

"Somewhere. That's what I was afraid of." The two men went into the living room where the farm records were kept in a file cabinet beside a rolltop desk. They both pulled up chairs and put their heads together over the books, moving a kerosene lamp closer since the day was dark and overcast.

Toby carried his empty coffee mug to the sink where Greta was scrubbing the dishes.

He slipped his cup into the soapy water. "For the first inning, I don't think it went too badly."

"Morris is only getting warmed up."

He sensed her anger boiling beneath the surface. Why did she let him get to her? "I noticed you didn't assure him that he was welcome."

She kept her eyes downcast as she began to wash the mug. "You told me I was a poor liar."

Toby wanted so badly to help her. "Greta, you have to forgive him. You are only hurting yourself by not doing so."

She whirled to face him, anger blazing in her eyes. She

slammed the cup on the counter so hard it broke. "Don't you think I know that!"

Activity in the kitchen stopped. Everyone gaped at her.

Chapter Twenty

Greta flushed hot with humiliation. She gathered the broken pieces of crockery and carefully stacked them on her palm. "I'm sorry. That was uncalled for."

She dropped the broken bits in the trash can, turned back to the sink and plunged her shaking hands into the soapy water.

"It's not the first time I've been yelled at," Toby said quietly.

"It's the first time you have been yelled at by me. You are right to point out my failings. I must work on them."

Naomi came up behind Greta. "Are you all right?"

Greta pasted a false smile on her face. "I'm just cranky. I guess I got up on the wrong side of the bed."

"It's okay, child. I understand that this is hard for you. Toby, why don't you see if Arles is ready for some breakfast?"

He left the kitchen and Greta was able to relax. "I shouldn't have yelled at him. He's a guest in your home."

"It's your home, too."

"It doesn't feel like it with *him* here."

Lizzie came to stand beside her. "By *him,* I assume you mean Morris and not Toby? What we hope to accomplish will not happen in a single day."

"I know that. I guess the problem is that I don't believe it will happen at all."

"Is that what all your book learning has told you?" Betsy asked.

Greta frowned. "What are you talking about?"

Betsy crossed her arms. "I've seen the books you bring home from the library in town and keep under your mattress. I know you've read a lot about this."

So her studies weren't as much a secret as she thought. She nodded. "I have read a lot about this subject. Sadly, abusers, unless they have a true desire to change, fall back into the same old pattern."

Betsy gripped Greta's arm. "Then we must pray that God will change our uncle's heart."

"You don't know how often I have prayed for that very thing. I've prayed for years." Greta's voice quivered. She wouldn't allow herself to cry.

Betsy hugged her. "We all have."

"And you think it has done no good?" Naomi asked.

Greta bowed her head. "I don't believe that. Prayer always does good. Even if you don't receive what you are asking for."

Naomi gathered all the girls into a hug. "If we pray to accept God's will, we will always be answered."

Greta laid her head against her step-grandmother's shoulder. "Have I been praying for the wrong thing?"

"Only you can answer that."

The rest of the day passed quickly. The women filled the hours with cooking and slipping away to secretly make small Christmas gifts for each other. Carl and Joe worked on the books, but Joe was constantly rising and going to the window. He wasn't used to being indoors. Greta knew he wanted to be out among the sheep.

Arles found a book from Carl's collection about Africa. As Carl had lived there briefly, he was able to answer Arles's many questions.

Greta felt Toby's eyes on her frequently. She knew he was still troubled by her outburst, but she had no way to reassure him in front of everyone. Finding any time alone together in the crowded house proved to be impossible. In the evening, Marianne took a book to Morris who was dozing in his chair. "Would you read to me?" she asked when he opened his eyes and looked at her.

Greta was ready to intervene if he became rude, but to her surprise, he sat up and took the book. "What do you have here, Miriam?"

"It's called *The Farm on Apple Creek*."

He opened the cover. "So it is. I read this when I was little, too."

Marianne pulled a chair over beside him and leaned on the arm of his chair as he turned the pages of the book and read to her.

Greta looked at her sisters. They were all as amazed as she was.

The blizzard raged through the night and showed no signs of stopping. The sound began to wear on everyone's nerves. Early the following morning, the women were gathered in the kitchen discussing the chores that needed to be done that day. Arles and Toby were upstairs. Carl and Joe were still working on the taxes with papers spread out around them. Naomi said, "Marianne, I need a favor."

"What?" The girl looked up with interest.

"I have several dozen Christmas cards I need to send yet, but I don't have any store-bought ones left. Would you help me make cards? I have scissors and glue and paper, I just haven't gotten around to starting them."

"I guess. I used to help *Mamm* make them at Christmastime.

"I can help, too," Greta offered. "Marianne, you will find some wrapping paper with birds and winter scenes on it in the desk in my room. Pick the ones you like and bring them down here."

"Okay." Marianne went running up the stairs.

Naomi rubbed her hands together. "*Goot.* After the dishes and morning chores are done, we will get our cards started. As soon as I find my list of people who still need cards. They might be late if the mail carrier can't get through, but no one will mind. They will have them well before Old Christmas."

Greta chuckled. January 6, Epiphany, was celebrated as Old Christmas by many Amish. Naomi and Joseph would keep it as a family day, with visiting and feasting, celebrating in much the same way as Christmas Day, but no gifts would be exchanged.

"What is the matter with that cat?" Betsy asked, looking toward the living room.

Greta heard Christmas meowing in the other room. She broke away from the group and went to investigate. Morris was sitting by the window staring out at the snow. Christmas paced back and forth in front of him meowing loudly.

"*Onkel,* are you okay?"

"Miriam doesn't like the snow, but I do," he said in a soft odd voice. He began rubbing his left arm.

"*Onkel,* where are your nitroglycerin pills?"

"In my room."

She rushed into his room and saw them on the night table. She snatched them up and hurried to his side. "Put one under your tongue."

"Why?" His blank face contorted with sudden pain. He curled forward and almost fell from the chair.

She caught him and held him up. Her grandfather and Carl jumped to their feet. Carl moved quickly to her side. "What's wrong?"

"He needs one of his pills. Help me sit him back."

Carl helped Morris sit back in the chair. Greta's hand

shook as she slipped a pill in his mouth. His face was contorted with pain and turned a ghastly pale color. There were beads of sweat on his forehead. Glancing over her shoulder, she said, "*Daadi,* bring him a glass of water."

Her grandfather hurried to the kitchen. When he returned, her sisters and Naomi followed him. "What's going on?" Naomi asked.

"*Onkel* Morris is having one of his angina attacks. The pill should help. If it doesn't, he can have another one in a few minutes. After that…" She let her voice trail off. If the pills didn't help, they would be unable to get him to a doctor.

Her family hovered around her. Slowly, Morris's contorted face began to relax. His color improved and his ragged breathing slowed. He opened his eyes. "Can you take a sip of water?" Greta asked.

He nodded weakly. She held the glass to his lips. He managed to swallow a little, then pushed it aside. "*Goot* Greta, *goot* little mouse."

For once, his words didn't sting. She rose to her feet. "With a cat and mouse in the house and by God's grace you may enjoy another day."

He sat up straighter. "Did the child see?"

"She's still upstairs."

"Why is everyone staring at me? Don't you have work to do?" He leaned back and closed his eyes.

Everyone but Greta returned to other parts of the house. Marianne came downstairs with her arms full of wrapping paper. She stopped at the bottom and looked around the room. "Where is my brother?"

"Behind you." Toby came down the stairs.

She looked up with relief. "I got scared when Christmas ran out of the room. I thought you were leaving."

Toby rubbed her head. "I can't go anywhere. There's a blizzard outside."

She gave him a sheepish grin. "I guess that's true. Where is Christmas?"

"She's with me," Morris said. The cat was now curled on his lap purring loudly.

"Will you watch her for me while I make Christmas cards with Naomi and Greta?"

"For a little while." Morris stroked the cat and stared out the window. He took another sip of water from the glass on the table.

"Danki." Marianne said cheerfully. Her voice, although hoarse, was stronger than it had been. "Greta, are these the papers you wanted me to use?"

"They are. Let's go in the kitchen." She glanced uneasily at Morris, but left the room, anyway. Her grandfather and Carl would keep an eye on him.

She set about gathering the things they would need to make Christmas cards. Toby stood beside her as she laid out the pieces of paper and the blank cards. After glancing around the room, he asked, "What's going on?"

"Onkel Morris had another attack."

"Is he okay?"

"I'm not sure. I think this was the worst one I have seen yet."

How many more could his damaged heart endure? How much time did he have left? Was he ready to face his Maker?

Naomi brought a box of crayons to the table. "Are you going to help us, Toby?"

"Sure, if you don't mind?"

"Not at all. I'm sure Greta will be thrilled to have your help."

Greta flashed Naomi an astonished look. What did she mean by that? Did she think there was something between them? The thought had no more crossed her mind before Naomi winked at her and whispered, "I like him."

Naomi turned to Betsy and Lizzie who were assembling ingredients for their baking marathon. "What shall we make first?"

The three women put their heads together over a recipe book, but when they looked up, they all looked at Greta and smiled before giggling and returning to the task. Surely Betsy was not spreading rumors about her and Toby? Greta's entire family was nuts. They all had romance on their minds.

When no one else was close enough to overhear, Toby stepped close to Greta. "Are we okay? You and me?"

His warm breath brushed her ear. Her heart started racing.

This foolishness had to stop. She was setting herself up for a serious case of heartache when he left.

He gazed into her eyes. "Are we?

Chapter Twenty-One

"We are okay. Well, you are. I still need some work." Greta gave Toby a shy smile that made his heart skip a beat.

"I think you are doing fine. Can I help make the cards?"

"Have you any artistic skills?"

"Not a one. I do know how to use scissors."

"Then you are welcome to join us, if it is okay with Marianne?" She looked over her shoulder at his sister laying out markers and crayons along with scissors at the far end of the table.

"Sure, you can help," she said. She looked up suddenly. "Unless you have something else you would rather do."

"And what would I rather do than make Christmas cards?"

She chewed her lip for a second. "It's kind of a girlie thing."

He held up both hands. "I draw the line at wearing a bonnet to do this."

She giggled. "That's just silly."

"That's me, silly Toby."

"*Daed* used to say silly things like that to make *Mamm* laugh."

Toby's heart twisted with pain. "He did, and she loved to laugh. I miss them, but I'm glad they are together."

"Me, too."

Greta sat down beside Marianne. "Why don't you make a Christmas card for them?"

Marianne looked up with a scowl. "We can't mail it."

"I know, but they can see it," Toby said, pleased with Greta's idea.

"Yeah, they can. Okay. This is *Mamm's* favorite color." Marianne reached for a blue card.

The next half hour was spent cutting out flowers and birds and gluing them on to the card stock. Greta drew a sheep on one and then glued cotton balls to it for fleece. Marianne was impressed.

Naomi wrote greetings and Bible verses inside each one and addressed the envelopes. Lizzie and Betsy were busy baking oatmeal cookies, and the kitchen was soon filled with delicious smells. Toby got up to sneak a few nibbles, but Lizzie laughingly chased him away with a wooden spoon.

They were nearing the end of Naomi's list when Carl and Joe came into the kitchen. Joe stopped beside Toby. "Would you care to come down to the barn and see our operation?"

"I'd like that. Marianne, you don't mind if I go with Joe and Carl, do you?"

She stopped coloring a rainbow over a farm. "You'll come back, won't you?"

"Sure."

"Okay. But don't be gone long."

"I won't." He was relieved that she agreed. She was getting over her complete dependence on him. Things might not have gone so well without Greta on this trip. He was more thankful than ever that the Lord saw fit to bring them together. Toby lifted his coat and hat off the peg by the front door.

"Just a minute," Greta said.

She left the room and came back a few moments later

with a heavy knitted gray scarf in her hands. "We wouldn't want your nose to freeze off."

She wrapped it around his neck. Her hands lingered briefly on his shoulders. Their eyes met. His world narrowed until the only thing in it was her beautiful face and the tenderness shining in her eyes. She was close enough to kiss.

Chapter Twenty-Two

How did she do that? How did she make his common sense fly out the window? He glanced at her family all watching him. He took a step back. "I'm ready."

Toby followed Joe and Carl outside. Duncan, Carl's ever-present shadow, came with them. The swirling white storm was disorienting. It was impossible to see more than a few feet in front of them. If not for the fence that led from the corner of the yard to the side of the barn, Toby wasn't sure they could've found their way. Although he was dressed for the weather, he was still surprised by the brutal cold.

He stepped inside the barn with a big sigh of relief and was sorry instantly. One thing Greta hadn't mentioned about sheep was the smell. They stank. And there were only half a dozen in the barn. What would it be like with nearly two hundred of them inside?

Carl pulled down his scarf and grinned at Joe. "It's good to be out of the house, isn't it?"

Joe grinned. "You can say that again. Sometimes I can't breathe in a closed-up space."

Toby thought of the delicious smells in the house and decided that shepherds were odd people if they would rather be out with these smelly creatures.

They soon had the sheep, the horses and the cows taken care of. Carl led the way to a newer section of the barn.

"This is our lambing shed. It has all the comforts of home. Propane-powered refrigerator for keeping frozen colostrum and milk substitute, propane heater to keep the place warm, a small stove to heat bottles and a couple of cots that we almost never use."

"Why so many small pens?" Toby surveyed the numerous compartments on either side of the main aisle. The area was much cleaner than the larger pens.

"All these small pens are for the orphan lambs or for grafting an orphan to a ewe that has lost a lamb or only has one."

"We doctor the sick ewes in here, too," Joe added.

"Do you get a lot of orphans?" Toby asked.

"We don't lose many ewes, but often an ewe with multiple lambs will only nurse one or two. We pen the ewe with the motherless lamb and hope she will nurse him. If she can't get away from the lamb, the little one's persistence to suckle can pay off. Sometimes it works, sometimes we end up bottle-feeding them."

Carl settled his hip on the wooden rail of one of the pens. "Sometimes we end up bottle-feeding a lot of them. I'm sorry you have been stranded with us, Toby. I wish there was some way we could let your family know that you are okay. It's a shame that your driver broke his phone."

"My aunt is a practical woman. She won't fret if we are a day or two late. Her oldest daughters work in a bakery in town. I can call and leave a message with them. How far away is your phone shack?"

"Too far to go in this weather. We must pray it breaks soon. If it doesn't, I will have a lot of buried sheep," Joe said.

"And that will not be fun," Carl added. "Greta is very taken with your little sister. I noticed they seem to have bonded."

Toby laughed. "Probably because they were shut together inside a space smaller than these orphan pens for two days."

"*Nee,* it is because she is a sweet child," Greta said from the doorway to the barn. "She is beginning to worry about you, Toby. I told her I would come and check on you."

"Then I should get back."

Carl stood. "Joe, you and I need to dig open the south doors so some of the ewes can get inside if they want."

"We should've done it before the snow got so deep. I doubt many of them are moving around."

"No one was prepared for this much snow in such a short period of time. We'll just have to do the best we can. Besides, there is a cedar tree outside the fence at that corner. If you can get through the drift, you can cut some branches for Naomi."

"The things I do for that woman." Taking a pair of grain shovels from hooks on the wall, the two men headed toward the south end of the building.

"I want to thank you for the card suggestion. It was a nice idea. I appreciate all you have done for my sister."

She clapped her hands together to knock the snow off of her gloves. "I wasn't much older than she is when I lost my parents. I understand what she's going through. What you are going through, too."

"I have accepted that it was God's will. What I don't understand is why Marianne had to suffer. I would give anything to have taken her place. I should have been there."

"God had a reason for that."

He settled his hip on the railing as Carl had done and folded his arms and admitted his shameful part in the tragedy. "I was out at a movie with my friends. My parents didn't even know I wasn't home. They had gone to bed and I was getting ready to do that when one of my buddies knocked on my window. They had a car waiting at the end of the lane and they had a date for me. I almost said no. I had to work the next day, but a few hours of fun sounded much better than a few hours of sleep. It wasn't even a good movie. I should have stayed home."

"It was not your time."

He stood up "I know that. If I had been there, Marianne might be alone now. God needs me to take care of her. We should go back to the house since she is worried. She is doing better at allowing me out of her sight, but I know how easily she can become frightened."

"You are good brother. God will bless you." She led the way back to the house.

When he walked inside, he found his sister sobbing and on the verge of hysterics. She ran toward him. He knelt to catch her. She threw her arms around him and held on tight enough to choke him. She didn't care that he was covered in snow.

"Marianne, stop it. I'm back. I told you I would be and I am. Calm down."

"I was worried. I couldn't see you. Don't go out again."

"I won't go out until it stops snowing and we can go home."

"Promise?" She drew back, wiped her nose on her sleeve and stared into his eyes.

"I promise. Can I have a smile now?"

"Not yet." She threw her arms around his neck again.

Toby managed to shed his coat with Naomi's help, then he lifted his sister in his arms and carried her into the living room. He sat down on the sofa with her in his lap. The cat left Morris to seek attention from Marianne.

"What was all the fuss about? Why are you blubbering like a baby?" Morris asked.

Marianne let go of Toby and wiped her face. "I'm not a baby." She pulled the cat into her lap.

"That's easy enough to see. So why are you crying like one?"

"I got scared."

"She gets frightened if I'm gone for too long," Toby explained.

"You shouldn't coddle her for such behavior. It makes her weak."

It was his guilt that made him coddle Marianne, Toby knew that. But he didn't know how else to respond to her needs. He noticed Greta watching them from the doorway to the kitchen. Her eyes told him of her sympathy. For himself, or for Marianne, he couldn't be sure which.

"I'm weak because I was in the hospital just like you," his sister told Morris.

"It was a miserable place, if you ask me." Morris turned back to the window.

"And as soon as we get you home, you will grow strong again," Toby assured her.

She scrubbed her face with her hands and nodded. "*Aenti* Linda said in her letters that I will get better quick as a wink when I get there. Can we go there soon? I want to go home."

Toby prayed that his aunt's words would prove true. He heard the outside door open. Greta glanced over her shoulder. It sounded as if Joe and Carl had come in. Toby leaned sideways to look at Marianne's face. "Are the tears done?"

Greta came to crouch in front of her. "If they are, you can help us put out the greenery. Would you like that?"

Greta held out her hand and helped Marianne scoot off Toby's lap. Naomi, Betsy and Lizzie came into the living room carrying fragrant bundles of cedar branches in a burlap sack. Marianne, her tears forgotten, helped them tie together the branches with cord to make a strand long enough to drape over the mantel.

Greta, smiling like a kid herself, tickled Marianne's good ear with the tip of a branch. Christmas, not wanting to be left out of the fun, began chasing the dangling end of the cord. Marianne giggled and teased the cat, making her dart left and right as she jiggled the other end.

"The snow will stop soon and you can take her home," Morris said.

Toby glanced at Morris, but his gaze was still fixed out the window. Looking back, he met Greta's gaze across the room. Toby realized with a jolt that he didn't want to leave. Pennsylvania was simply too far away from the woman he couldn't get off his mind. A smile lifted the corner of his mouth. "I hope it snows for a month of Sundays."

Greta rolled out of bed the next morning and drew back the curtains. It was still snowing. Possibly harder than it had the day before.

He wouldn't be leaving today. She grinned, rubbed her hands together and turned around to find Betsy watching her.

Her sister arched one eyebrow. "Okay, what's going on?"

Greta composed her face. She glanced at Marianne's bed and saw the child was still sleeping. She lowered her voice. "I don't know what you mean."

Betsy spoke softly, too. "No one is that happy to see a blizzard this close to Christmas."

Greta went to the closet and pulled out a lavender dress with a black apron. It wasn't her best dress, that one was reserved for Sunday services, but it was her second best. Much nicer than her worn and stained everyday garments. "I like snow."

"No you don't. I think you're grinning because one certain guest will be staying a few more days."

Unable to keep her happiness contained, Greta glanced over her shoulder at Betsy. "Does it show?"

"To someone who doesn't know you well, maybe not. To your sister, it shows."

Greta crossed the room to sit on the bed beside Betsy. "It's foolish, isn't it?"

"It's not going to snow forever," Betsy said gently.

Greta picked at a loose thread on the quilt. "I know. But it's snowing today and I'm going to be thankful for that. He makes me laugh. Sometimes, he seems to know what I'm thinking. Odd, isn't it?"

Betsy pulled the covers back to her chin. "It's too early to be up. Go back to sleep."

"Betsy, can I ask you a question?"

"If you must. Then will you go back to sleep?"

"Are you in love with Alvin?"

Flipping the quilt down, Betsy folded her arms and studied the ceiling. "I think we will get there. We are comfortable with each other. We like the same things. We want the same things. He's a good man."

"But if you don't love him, surely you aren't thinking of marriage?" Greta reached out to take Betsy's hand.

"I am thinking about it, but I'm young and I'm not in any hurry to settle down. Enough about me, what about your new fellow? He's good-looking. I love his smile and that dimple!"

Greta returned to pulling at the loose thread. "They'll be leaving soon. He has a sister to take care of. You saw how she was when he was outside."

"Poor Marianne. She has had a lot of sorrow for one so young. Have you noticed how taken with her our uncle is? He never treated us so kindly."

"That's true, but if she can reach him, our uncle is not beyond hope. Betsy, have you forgiven him?"

"I have forgiven him, but I have not forgotten his cruelty. What about you?"

"I have not forgotten or forgiven. I think God must be very disappointed in me."

"I think God is much more disappointed with *Onkel*

Morris. It's cold up here. I think I hear Naomi in the kitchen. Let's get downstairs so you can make sheep eyes at Toby and I can warm my toes by the fire."

"I haven't been making sheep eyes at him."

"I don't know what else you would call it."

"Have I really? Do you think he noticed?"

Betsy began to dress quickly. "I don't see how he could miss it because he's always making sheep eyes at you, too."

"Is he?" That giddy sensation returned in full force. She couldn't help but smile. She closed her eyes to hold the feeling close.

When she opened them, she saw Betsy's smile had faded. Her expression grew serious. "Greta, are you falling for Toby?"

Some of her happiness fled. "I don't know. Maybe."

"Oh, please, don't."

"Why do you say that?" She thought Betsy would understand.

"If you have to ask, I'm really worried. I thought you were just having some fun, a little flirtation. You've only known him a few days. Days! Do you hear what I'm saying? He's going to be gone as soon as the snow lets up. He lives hundreds of miles away. Do you think he'll come courting on Saturday evenings or after Sunday services?"

Why did her sister have to make it sound so hopeless? "I know he won't. But I'm happy when I'm with him. Is that so bad?"

Betsy sighed. "It isn't bad, but don't lose your head. Or your heart. Be sensible, Greta. Please."

"I will," she said, but was it already too late?

Chapter Twenty-Three

Greta slipped back under the covers. So what if it was foolish to crave another day of Toby's company. She couldn't help it. She couldn't. She was foolishly falling head over heels for him. He would leave soon, but not today.

Not today. I won't be sensible today. He won't leave today. Please, God, let it snow a few days longer.

She would be sensible when Toby was gone, but not until then.

Marianne was still asleep, but Betsy had gone downstairs. With Naomi and Betsy both in the kitchen, there was no need for Greta to rush down. She sat up abruptly. Except that Toby might be up already, and she would be free to visit with him.

Tossing back the heavy quilts, she quickly put up her hair and pulled on her lavender dress. When she opened the door, Christmas came in. She stooped to pet the cat. "Happy morning, little one. The day you are named for is almost here. We should make it your official birthday and have a celebration for you, too."

Although she felt like skipping down the stairs, Greta maintained a sedate pace. Her uncle Morris was reading by the fireplace. Although she worried that he would ruin her good mood, she called out, "Good morning, *Onkel*. I hope you're feeling well this fine day."

"There's nothing fine about it. The cold is seeping into these old bones. I will soon be as stiff as an icicle."

Yes, he was all doom and gloom, but it didn't affect Greta's mood one bit. Toby was sitting on the couch reading a book. His friendly smile warmed her heart as he wished her a good morning. She entered the kitchen still floating on a cloud of happiness.

Not today. He wouldn't leave today.

She stopped when she saw her grandfather pacing back and forth in front of the kitchen window. The wind howled outside unabated. She knew from the look on his face that he was deeply worried.

Carl was facing the window, too. "I built a half dozen sheds in the pastures for them this fall. Most of them will weather this storm safely."

"You did a fine job, but they won't all go into the sheds. Sheep are funny that way. Some of them will shelter along the stone walls or in the thickets. Those are the ones that I'm worried about."

"If the snow drifts over them, will they smother?" Greta asked. She had been so happy to see the snow. She had prayed for it to continue. Now she saw the folly of her selfish prayers.

Her grandfather turned to look at her. "They can smother, but often they huddle together and the heat of their bodies will form air holes to the surface. I'm more worried that the pregnant ewes won't find enough feed. If they can paw down and can get to grass, they can survive for a few days, but if they can't move, they will start to starve and that may cause them to miscarry. They need good feed to have healthy lambs. I pray God watches over them all."

"And that's all you can do at this point, Joseph," Naomi said from her place by the stove where she and Betsy were cooking. "Worrying will not help them. It shows a lack of faith in God's mercy."

Daadi turned away from the window. "You're right. The storm is by His will. Whatever comes of it is meant to be."

Naomi smiled at him. "Invite our guests to breakfast and then you should have a game of checkers. I'm sure one of them will take you on."

Greta's grandfather moved to his place at the table. "I hope it's Morris. I would love to give him a sound beating."

Naomi crossed her arms as she gave him a stern look.

"At checkers, my good wife. I was talking about beating him at checkers."

"Sure you were. Greta, call the others. The girls and I have many things to bake. Christmas will be here before we know it and I want to be ready. I don't need a bunch of men in my kitchen today."

"It's my kitchen, too, you know," *Daadi* said. "It was my kitchen for twenty years before you showed up."

"And how many Christmas cookies did you bake in all that time? Well?" she demanded when he stayed silent.

He hooked his thumbs under his suspenders. "Not many."

"None, I would venture to say. So if you want a delicious assortment this year, go play checkers in the other room after breakfast or put on an apron."

"If I had known how bossy you were, I would've thought twice about asking you to marry me."

She walked up to him and gave him a peck on the cheek. "You never did ask me. I'm the one who proposed because you never had the courage. Tell the truth, now, Joseph."

"*Ja,* you proposed. Then, quick as a wink, I was shackled."

She chuckled. "And how many days have you regretted that?"

He tapped her nose with his finger. "Not one single

hour. I like snickerdoodles. I like chocolate chip cookies and I like the ones you make with the cherries in the center."

"My thumbprint cookies?"

"*Ja,* those."

"Then you shall have all three if you stay out of my kitchen today and let me cook."

"I will, I will," he grumbled. "Can I have my breakfast now?"

Greta went up to wake Marianne, but the girl was already up. When they came back downstairs, everyone else was already seated at the table. Although the food was plentiful, hot and delicious, everyone's mood was subdued. When they finished eating, her grandfather leaned back in his chair. "Who is up for a quick game of checkers this morning?"

"Marianne likes to play checkers," Toby said with a smile for his sister.

Naomi began gathering up plates. "There you go, Joe. Play a game of checkers with Marianne. It will do her good to play someone she can beat."

He laughed as he left the room with Toby and Marianne. Naomi's smile faded as she watched them. She moved to stare out the window, crossing her arms as if she were cold.

Greta joined her. "You are good to distract him."

"I don't like to see him worry. I pray this storm ends soon and that God intends to save our sheep. I'm not sure Joseph has it in him to start over."

"I will pray it ends soon, too." Greta's gaze was drawn to the living room where the game table was being set up. Toby had pulled a chair over to sit beside his sister. He noticed Greta's gaze, smiled at her and winked. She smiled back, but her heart was heavy. Their time together couldn't go on forever. He would leave and she would be left to wonder if it could have turned into something more for them.

More than a brief flirtation.

That's all it was. She might wish it were more, but she had to be practical. Betsy was right to caution her. She would not lose her head or her heart to someone she had known less than a week. Love at first sight was the stuff of *Englisch* romance novels that she and her sisters had read on the sly when they were teenagers.

Real love had to grow over months and even years of getting to know each other. It took time and prayer to know if that person was the mate God had chosen for you.

Toby, acutely aware of Greta's sadness, wondered at the cause as the day wore on. She worked very hard at hiding it from others, but sometimes he would catch her when she thought no one was looking. The storm had everyone on edge, but he knew it was more than that. He hated seeing her unhappy. It wasn't until late in the day that he managed to get her alone. Naomi sent her to the cellar to bring up jars of canned fruit. Toby put his book down and said, "Let me help you."

It seemed for a moment as if she would refuse him, but then she nodded. He followed her down the steep steps to the basement. She switched on two battery-operated lanterns that hung at the foot of the stairs. The dark recesses were bathed in sudden light. Tables and benches were stored along one wall along with an assortment of summer lawn furniture. The other walls were lined with floor-to-ceiling shelving that housed hundreds of jars full of produce.

She walked along the shelves pulling out jars of peaches, blueberries and plums. She handed them to him and tried to reach a jar of quinces. It was just out of her reach.

"Let me get that for you." He stepped up.

"I can manage." She rose on tiptoe. She was still an inch shy of her goal.

"I can manage, too," he said, stepping in beside her. Their shoulders brushed against each other. She took a quick step away. He handed her the jar of fruit.

"Danki." She wouldn't look at him.

"Greta, are we still okay?" He asked, wondering if he had done something to upset her.

She turned away. "Your family in Pennsylvania must be worried by now. I'm sure you'll be glad to get back to them."

"Of course I will."

"The storm can't last much longer."

"You don't think it will snow for another month of Sundays?"

She turned back to the shelves. "I hope not. *Daadi* is very worried about his sheep. They can't do without food much longer in this cold."

"It's hard to remember that other creatures are suffering while we are snug and warm."

Naomi came to the top of the stairs. "Are you having trouble finding something?"

The mother hen checking on her chick. Toby smiled at the image, but he understood her concern.

"The quince, but I have it now." Greta ran up the steps leaving Toby to turn off the lights. He still didn't have a clue what was wrong. He was only halfway up when Betsy appeared in the doorway above him. He stepped aside to let her pass, but she stopped a few risers up.

"You might think that Greta is tough, but she isn't. She is the frailest of my sisters. She has scars you can't see. I was happy to see her enjoying a little flirtation until I realized that wasn't the case. She likes you, but unless you are planning to stay in our community, be careful. Don't make her wish for something she can't obtain. She has had failure thrown in her face far too many times."

He stared at her in surprise. "I like your sister, too. I honestly do."

"I'm glad, but that isn't enough. I'll take those jars."

He handed them over. She smiled. "*Danki* for your help. I'm glad we had this little talk." She trotted up the steps and closed the door, leaving him in the dark.

So the women of the family were banding together to protect Greta from the big bad wolf. He'd never pictured himself in that role. Were they right to worry? Was this connection he shared with Greta doing her harm?

That was the last thing he wanted.

So what should he do about it?

Greta pleaded a headache and spent the rest of the day in her bedroom. It was the coward's way out, but she didn't know what else to do. Facing Toby only made things worse. She didn't know how to explain what was wrong. That she had foolishly allowed herself to become infatuated with him. So rather than pretend indifference, she was hiding in her cold bedroom working on her cross-stitching with gloves on her hands. She spent as much time pulling out her mistakes as she did completing a pattern.

When Betsy and Marianne came up at bedtime, Greta was already under the covers pretending to be asleep. Sometime in the middle of the night, she woke listening for the wind, but all she heard was silence. She went to the window, but the glass was frosted over and she couldn't see out.

Quietly, she donned her robe and slippers and went downstairs. She padded silently through the kitchen. At the front door, she pulled on her coat and stepped out onto the porch. The storm was gone. The air was calm and crystal clear. Millions of stars sparkled in the black sky and lent their glitter to the snowy white fields. Her breath rose in frosty puffs in the still night air.

"It seems the storm has blown itself out."

Greta's heart gave a happy leap at the sound of Toby's voice before she forced it to be calm. She turned to see him standing in the doorway. The only light came from the glow of the snowy fields and the stars. She couldn't see his face, but she knew every inch of it. "I'm sorry if I woke you."

"You didn't. I think it was the silence. After so many days of wind, it was eerie."

"That's what woke me, too." She pulled her coat tightly over her chest. "You'll be able to leave soon."

He came to stand beside her. "I should be happy, but I'm not."

"Why aren't you?" The darkness made her bold. If she couldn't see his face, then he couldn't see what was in her eyes. A fierce longing to be held in his arms.

"If the storm is over, the roads will be cleared and we will be on our way to Pennsylvania again."

"Isn't that what you wanted?"

He reached out to cup her cheek. "It was before I met you."

She should pull away. A single step back would be enough to tell him he had gone too far, but she didn't take that step. Her heart thudded painfully as she tried to make light of their time together. "We shared an adventure, Toby. That's all it was."

The pad of his thumb brushed over her lips. "*Nee,* this was much more than an adventure. For the first time in my life, I see my heart's desire. It's true we haven't known each other very long—"

"You don't know me at all, Toby. Not really."

"But I want to, Greta. I want to know everything about you."

"And what if you don't like what you discover?"

"I don't see how that's possible."

"This has to stop, Toby. We don't have a future." She turned her head away from his hand. He let his arm drop to his side.

"I've spent all day trying to figure out a way to stop caring for you. I can't. I only see one option. I've decided to stay in Hope Springs."

Her gaze snapped to his face, but it was too dark to read his expression. "What did you say?"

Chapter Twenty-Four

Toby wanted to gather Greta in his arms. He heard the uncertainty in her voice. What he wanted to hear was joy. Didn't she want him to stay?

"I've decided to remain in the Hope Springs area. I'll find work here, and put down roots. Hopefully, someone will have use for a wood-carver. If not, I'll find something. I know this might offend you, but I don't think I can raise sheep. They stink."

"No, they don't. But what about your family? What about Marianne? Do you think she will want to stay here?"

"I think if we give her a little time, she will come to love it here. She is already fond of you and your family. As for my family in Pennsylvania, they will have to understand."

Toby didn't kid himself, his aunt would not like this, but she would come to accept it in time.

"It's such a big decision. You should think it over. I don't want you to do this for me. What if this attraction we have isn't real?"

"I agree that it's a big decision, and I agree I need to think about it and pray about it." He cupped her face between his hands. "Greta, God brought me here for a reason. I think the reason is you. I'm not going to leave, so we can take our time and get to know each other. If it isn't right, I want to know that, too. Don't you?"

"I'm not sure."

"What do you mean?"

"I think it might be better to believe it was real but that you had to go away than know it wasn't real."

"The truth is the truth, Greta. It is neither good nor ill. I think this is real, and I'm going to stick around until you know it is real. Now, we should go inside, it's freezing out here and smart people are in bed this time of night."

"At least the storm is over and we can find the lost sheep as soon as it is light."

"Oh, joy. More time with smelly sheep." She giggled and his heart soared.

Greta couldn't sleep a wink. Toby wasn't leaving.

It was what she wanted, wasn't it? Of course it was.

She pushed aside the small nagging grain of doubt that told her he had made this decision too quickly. He was a grown man. He was capable of making his own choices. Marianne would grow to love the community the way Greta and her sisters had.

The storm was over and Toby wasn't leaving. That was all she cared about.

Naomi came to her room at first light. "Dress warmly, girls. We have a lot of sheep to find."

The family assembled in the kitchen shortly after dawn. Greta and Betsy, Carl, Joseph and Toby were dressed in layers of clothing and heavy overshoes. Naomi and Lizzie would stay at the house with Marianne, Morris and Arles.

Carl addressed the group. "We're going to use Duncan to help us locate our missing sheep. We assume they are buried under the snow. I have already checked the shelters and have a head count. We have at least thirty unaccounted for. The sooner we can get to them, the better their chances of survival."

"What do you need me to do?" Toby asked.

"We will work together in pairs. Duncan and I will locate a likely area and leave two of you to dig them out. The other two will come with us while we look for another pocket of animals. Pace yourselves. Shoveling snow is hard work. If any of the animals are showing signs of distress, try to get them to the barn. I have shovels for everyone on the porch. Are we ready?"

They all nodded and headed out the door. Toby moved beside Greta. "What does a distressed sheep look like?"

"Let's hope you don't have to find out."

They walked out into a world blanketed in brilliant white silence. Every surface was covered with snow. The trees were weighted down with it, their drooping branches pulled almost to the ground. Every fence post wore a white hat. The glittering brightness of the fields against the brilliant blue sky was breathtaking.

Together, they trudged across the pasture, sometimes breaking through the snow crust, sometimes able to walk along the top of it. The landscape was so changed by the drifts of snow that Greta wasn't certain where the stone fences lay. Duncan worked back and forth at Carl's command, searching for any sheep hidden under the snow.

A few hundred yards beyond the barn, Duncan stopped and began digging. Carl pulled him aside. Toby dug down and hit a stone wall. The snow caved in six inches to the left of it and a sheep's muzzle appeared. Carl patted Duncan. "Good boy. Keep count of the ones that you free. We'll compare totals when we regroup at noon."

Her grandfather and Betsy followed Duncan and Carl as they went on. Greta and Toby worked to enlarge the opening in the snow until he could reach in and pull the reluctant sheep out. A second and a third animal followed of their own accord. The animals staggered through the deep snow toward the barn.

"Three. It's a start," Greta said.

He leaned on his shovel. "That's all we need, isn't it? A start?"

She knew he wasn't talking about the sheep. She smiled and allowed happiness to rise in her chest. "A start and God's helping hand. The rest is up to us."

"I see Carl waving. I think he's found some more."

They began trudging through the snow toward a group of trees with limbs sagging to the ground under their load of white. "You don't really think sheep stink, do you?" Greta asked.

"I don't wish to speak ill of them."

She laughed. "You get used to it."

"You're talking to a man who carves fragrant cedar and sweet apple wood. I don't think I'll get used to the smell, but I can put up with it."

Although it was the hardest day's work that Greta had ever done, she had never enjoyed anything more than working beside Toby. Naomi and Marianne brought them hot coffee and tea in the morning. At noon, they came in to warm up with hot soup and sandwiches. Marianne seemed at ease being without her brother although Naomi told them the child had stayed glued to the upper story windows in order to keep watch on them.

The lines of stress around Greta's grandfather's eyes disappeared when Carl announced their final tally just before dark. They'd found all the missing sheep. Only one was sick enough to need extra care, but Carl was optimistic about her chances of recovery.

As they filed into the house, Marianne flew to her brother and threw her arms around him. "You're safe. It was getting dark and I was worried."

"You are very brave to stay with Naomi while we found the missing sheep. We saved them all, aren't you glad?"

"Does this mean we can go home now?"

Greta met Toby's gaze over his sister's head and read

the hesitancy in his eyes. He leaned away from his sister to look her in the eyes. "Not yet, *lieschen*. We're going to be here a little while longer."

The nagging grain of doubt came back to rub against Greta's happiness. Was Toby doing the right thing for the right reason?

It was noon the next day when Duncan suddenly ran to the door and began barking. Greta looked out but didn't see anything. She opened the door and stepped onto the porch. In the distance, she heard the faint jingle of sleigh bells. Duncan raced down the lane barking a welcome.

The sound of the bells grew louder. She stepped inside the house. "Arles, I think your tow truck may be coming."

"I haven't had a chance to call for one. How can that be?"

"Come see."

Her brother-in-law, Ethan Gingerich, was driving his huge team of Belgian draft horses up the lane. Four abreast, the caramel-colored animals with blond manes and tails leaned into their collars as they pulled a snowplow, raising flurries of powder with every step. Off to one side, a colt running free frolicked alongside his working mother. Ethan stood on a platform just in front of the blade. Behind him, on a separate platform, stood Clara and the children all clinging to a large steering wheel that could change the angle of the blade.

The children waved when they caught sight of Greta. She waved back. Ethan didn't pause. He sent the team in several wide loops around the yard clearing a path between the house and the barns. Only when he was finished with the job did he stop the team. Clara and the children climbed down, their faces rosy with the cold.

"Go in the house, children, and warm up. I imagine

Naomi can whip up some hot chocolate and cookies." Clara sent her brood inside.

Smiling brightly, Clara clasped Greta's hands. "I'm so happy to see you. How was your trip?" She glanced toward the house, and her smile dimmed. "How is *Onkel* Morris? And who are those people?"

Toby and Arles were watching from the porch. Greta didn't see Marianne. She made the introductions and then said, "Go inside and warm up, Clara. I will tell you everything, but first I must speak to Ethan."

Greta walked out to Ethan who was checking over his team and patting each one as a reward for their hard work. "Good morning, Ethan. I have another job for you if your team is up for it."

"I'm glad to see you made it safely home before the storm. Clara was worried. A few minutes rest and my team will be ready for anything. What do you need?"

"Ethan, this is Arles Hooper and Toby Yoder. Arles is the driver who brought me home. His van ran off the highway north of our lane and hit the stone wall by the creek the night the snow started. Do you think you could see about pulling him out?"

"I reckon I could. Even if we get you out, the highway hasn't been plowed so you aren't going anywhere. Some of the drifts are five feet high."

Arles nodded. "I figured it would take a day or two. I doubt my van will run, but I sure would feel better having it somewhere safe."

"Dress warm and we will go see what can be done."

"Bless you, Ethan." Greta waved.

"Mind if I come, too?" Toby asked from the porch. He was slipping into his coat.

Ethan motioned him to come on. "I never turn down extra help."

Toby stopped beside Greta. "I figure I should meet all the family. Do you mind?

"Not at all."

Arles came out with his coat on. Marianne came rushing out behind him. "Wait for me. I want to come, too."

Toby shook his head. "I'm going to help pull Mr. Hooper's van out of the ditch."

Greta said, "You should stay here and visit with the children who just arrived. The men have work to do."

"I don't want to talk to the kids. I want to go with Toby."

Greta glanced at Toby, expecting him to second her suggestion and insist Marianne stay home. Toby looked to Ethan. "Do you mind?"

Toby knew he should have insisted Marianne stay at the house. Working around big horses pulling heavy loads could be risky, but he didn't want Marianne to make a scene in front of Greta's family.

Thankfully, the job turned out to be easier than he thought. It took less than ten minutes for Ethan's Belgian team to pull the crippled vehicle out of its snow-covered grave once they located it.

Arles walked around the front of it, brushing off the snow, and looking over the damage with an assessing eye. "It may not be as bad as I thought, but it sure is gonna need some work before it's roadworthy."

Ethan handed the reins to Toby and joined Arles. "Would you like me to tow it back to the farm, or do you want to leave it here?"

"How long do you think it will take to get a tow truck out here?"

"The county plows the road between here and Hope Springs pretty quickly. Depending on how many other cars are in the ditches, I'd say maybe late today or early tomorrow."

"Where did you say that phone booth is?"

"Hop on, I'll take you there. It's about a quarter of a mile up the road."

Toby was familiar with shared telephones located between Amish farms. Often solar powered, they normally contained a phone and a message machine. Amish farmers could contact feed stores and produce buyers with a minimum of interruption in their workday. The landowners around the phone shared the expense of its upkeep, but no one would claim to own it.

Ethan pulled the horses to a stop in front of the booth. A small gray building not much bigger than a closet sat back from the road near a cluster of trees. As Toby expected, a solar panel extended out from the south side of the roof. If there was a path to the door, it was obscured by drifts of snow. At least the booth itself was accessible.

Marianne, her cheeks red with the cold, pointed to the phone booth. "Are you going to talk to *Aenti* Linda?" The cold made her voice hoarse, too.

"Not unless *Aenti* Linda happens to be at the bakery. Elsa and Karen should be working there today. They can give our aunt a message, but Mr. Hooper needs to use the phone first."

Toby waited with his sister and Ethan while Arles made his call. Toby looked Greta's brother-in-law up and down. A mountain of a man, he almost matched his horses in size. "I understand you recently wed Greta's sister. May God smile on your union."

"*Danki,* I was a blessed man the day Clara showed up on my farm with my troublesome nephew in tow. She could see that I had no idea what to do with my brother's three children. It was fortunate for me that she decided to take us all under her wing."

"How does she feel about her uncle coming to stay?"

"She was not thrilled, but she will do everything she

can for him. He made their lives a misery. It has taken a lot for her to find forgiveness in her heart. I imagine it's the same for the others. The good Lord causes our lives to take some very strange turns."

"That He does," Toby said, thinking of all that had changed in his life and was about to change again.

Arles tromped through the snow on the way back from the phone. "They will have a tow truck out here by two o'clock. He said the snowplow is headed this way now. I'll ride into town with a tow truck so the mechanic and I can look her over together. I don't trust just anyone with my livelihood."

Having a ride was too good an opportunity to pass up. The sooner he got to town, the sooner Toby could start looking for work. "Do they have a general store in town?"

Ethan nodded. "MacGregor runs a nice grocery there."

"Do you think your tow truck driver would mind another passenger?" Toby asked. He could pick up some things he needed and ask around about work at the same time.

"Don't see why not." Arles climbed up on the platform behind Ethan. Toby and Marianne trudged to the phone booth. He placed a quick call to the bakery where his nieces worked. The girls were overjoyed to hear that he and Marianne were safe. He watched his sister's expression light up at the sound of their voices when he allowed her to talk to them for a little while. Finally, he took the receiver back. "I have no idea when we will get there. Our van is wrecked and we don't know how long before it can be fixed. There are some other things going on, too, so tell your mother not to expect us for Christmas. I'll let you know as soon as I know something for certain."

He cut short their chitchat with the promise to call again before Christmas and then he hung up.

Marianne sighed deeply. "I wish we could be there for Christmas."

"We'll have a nice Christmas here. I promise."

"I know, but it won't be the same."

They rejoined Ethan and Arles at the snowplow and Ethan took them back to the farm to await the arrival of the snowplow and tow truck.

Greta came out onto the porch to greet them when they stopped in front of the gate. Toby's heart swelled with happiness at the sight of her. He had made the right decision. They deserved a chance to find out if what they shared was love. For his part, he was growing more convinced by the hour. But was she?

Chapter Twenty-Five

It took some convincing on Greta's part, but she finally got Marianne to agree to stay at the farm while Toby went into town. As soon as he was out the door, the child stuck to Greta's side like a cocklebur.

All of the sisters were seated around the kitchen table with Naomi when Clara's oldest, eight-year-old Micah, came up to Marianne. "*Daadi* Joseph says we can build a snowman in his yard. Do you want to come help us?"

Greta gave Marianne a little shake. "That sounds like fun. Go on. You don't want to sit here and listen to us gossip, do you?"

Marianne slowly rose to her feet and followed the boy. Greta watched them from the living room window for a while. After a few hesitant minutes, Marianne got into the spirit of the adventure. It soon became a contest between the girls and the boys. Marianne and four-year-old Lily were rolling and patting together a ball of snow while Micah and five-year-old Amos tried to roll a bigger one faster.

"It looks like Marianne enjoys the snow," Clara said.

That brought to mind something Morris had said earlier. Greta returned to the kitchen. "Naomi, I know Morris lived in this area before the family moved to Indiana when I was little. Does the name Miriam mean anything to you?"

"I've known a few women with that name, why?"

"Because Morris sometimes calls Toby's sister by that name. He has such a faraway look in his eyes when he does. It's like he is talking to someone from the past." He was napping at the moment and all of them hoped he would stay in his room.

"Miriam. Oh, yes, I believe he had a sister by that name. She was a few years younger than the boys. Your mother told me about her. She died when she was ten I think. If I remember right, your mother said that she was always sickly. My memory isn't what it used to be, but I'm sure Bishop Zook would know. He has all the records of births and deaths in this community, although that would have been before his time, too, but the previous bishop would have kept those records."

"Or you could ask Morris." Clara motioned toward the living room with her head. He was up and moving to his usual chair by the window.

Greta hesitated. "I'm not sure I want to do that." While he hadn't been overtly cruel, his sarcasm never let up.

"He is the one person who can tell you for sure," Lizzie said, always one to get right to the point.

"Maybe he would like to talk about her," Naomi said. "When we reach the golden years of our lives, our minds are often drawn back into the past. Things were better then. We were younger and stronger. Summers were longer. The snow wasn't as cold. The people we knew back then gain a new importance to us. Morris might want to reminisce about her. You should ask him."

Greta saw her uncle watching Marianne and the other children playing in the snow. She gathered her courage and approached him. "Did you like playing in the snow when you were that age, too?"

"What boy doesn't?"

"What about Miriam?"

"She never liked the snow. It wasn't good for her. Do you think she should come in? I don't want her to catch her death."

"Is that what happened to Miriam?"

He turned and scowled at Greta. He sat in the chair and looked up at her. "Why all these questions?"

"We never knew each other very well. I would like to change that."

"Because I'm dying?"

Greta sat on the footstool by the chair and wrapped her arms around her knees. "You are part of my family. I didn't even know I had an aunt until I asked Naomi about it. I've heard you call Marianne Miriam a number of times. I knew the name meant something to you. Can you tell me about her?"

"She died. What is there to tell?" He stared out the window.

"I'm sorry she died, but she lived, too. That's important to me. I shall meet her in heaven one day, and it will be good to know something about her. Naomi thought she was a sickly child, is that true?"

"My mother coddled her. It made her weak. My father thought he could make her stronger, but she died, anyway. My mother cried for so long, but father couldn't stand the sound. He would hit her to make her stop. He said the world was a cruel place and only the strong survived in it. It was his job to make us strong. Sometimes I hated him, but he made me strong. I tried to make you girls strong, but what good did it do? You turned against me."

For the first time, Greta realized that Morris had been an abused child. In her reading on the subject, she learned it was often a cycle passed from parent to child, but she'd never considered that he might be a victim, too. "I'm sorry."

He glared at her. "For what?"

"For the loss of your sister and the pain your father caused you. Thank you for telling me about Miriam." She rose and left the room.

Toby returned from town with a good lead on a job and two pretty wooden boxes in a brown paper bag. He had purchased them at a gift shop that catered to *Englisch* tourists by selling Amish-made products. The boxes were plain walnut, but he had an idea to carve a scene in each lid and give them as Christmas gifts to Marianne and Greta.

"It will take at least three days to get the van fixed," Arles said with a sad shake of his head at supper that evening. "It won't be ready until the day after Christmas."

"All that means is that you will be with us for Christmas," Naomi said brightly. Tomorrow was Christmas Eve.

"I surely do hate to impose at the holidays like this. I plan to move into the inn in town. They have room for me. Nothing against your hospitality, but I would feel better staying there."

Naomi waved her hand back and forth. "Nonsense. It's no imposition at all. We are happy to have you. The Lord sent you to us and we will do our best to make up for missing Christmas with your own family."

"I don't have any family to speak of. The wife and I got divorced years ago. She took our two girls and moved to California. They are grown now and they lead busy lives. I only see them in the summer."

"I'm sorry to hear this. Having our family with us is a wonderful gift at Christmastime. You must come with us to the school program tomorrow. *Englisch* guests are welcome. You will enjoy watching the children put on their plays, sing songs and recite poetry. It will lift your spirits, for that is what God wishes for us at this time of year."

"That's mighty nice of you to invite me."

Naomi turned to Marianne and Toby. "And you must join us, too."

Marianne pressed her hand to her cheek and shook her head. "I don't want to go. People will stare at me."

"What will they see when they look at you?" Greta asked. She cocked one eyebrow at the girl as she waited for her to answer.

"Someone who is ugly."

Greta nodded. "I reckon you're right if you think that."

"Greta!" Toby chided. "My sister is not ugly."

"I did not say she was. Does anyone here think Marianne is an ugly child? Speak up. I don't hear anyone agreeing with her."

Marianne turned a fierce scowl at Greta. "They don't have to say it. I know it."

"You do look different, Marianne. Different, not ugly. People may stare at you because they are surprised or because they feel sorry that something bad happened to you. Not because they think you're ugly. If you don't want to go, we understand. We don't want you to feel uncomfortable. We want you to come with us because we enjoy being with you. You—exactly the way you are. And we want you to have fun, too. We won't be mad at you if you decide to stay home. We appreciate your being honest about it." Greta waited for his sister to speak.

Marianne looked to Toby. "Do you think I should go?"

"I do. You are a strong person inside. If we were in Pennsylvania, you would go to your cousins' program, wouldn't you?"

"I guess." She touched her large black bonnet and looked at Greta. "Could you make me a *kapp* like yours? One they can't see through?"

"Of course," Greta agreed. "I can even make it black."

Toby shared a warm glance with Greta. Thanks to her, his sister was making wonderful strides. He didn't know what her family would think of his change of plans. He wanted to have a job lined up and an idea of where he could live before he made that announcement. For now, it was enough to see Marianne opening up, showing her what life here could be like. He would have to tell Marianne and his family about his decision soon, though. What would her reaction be?

Early in the afternoon on Christmas Eve, Greta's family gathered outside on the porch and waited for Carl and her grandfather to arrange blankets and warm bricks in the large sleigh. Naomi fairly danced with anticipation. Greta only had eyes for Toby. She could hardly wait to ride to school, snuggled at his side in the sleigh. Joe waved them to come on when he had things arranged to his satisfaction.

Betsy and Lizzie were chatting happily. Toby and Carl helped everyone in. Naomi settled up front with Joe. They let Marianne sit between them. Greta found herself squeezed between Betsy and Toby while Lizzie and Carl shared the backseat.

Joe turned around to look at everyone. "Are we ready?"

Marianne grabbed his arm. "Wait, where is Morris?"

"He has decided to stay at home. We should get going. We don't want to be late. I haven't been to school in fifty years."

It was well-known in the community that Joseph Shetler was something of a hermit. It wasn't until Carl King showed up and started working for him that Joe opened up even a little. It took the arrival of his granddaughters and the persistent courting of Naomi to finally break through the shell around his heart. Once that wall came down, he became a new man.

The ride to the school took less than half an hour. Toby held Greta's hand beneath the quilt that covered them. She couldn't remember ever being happier.

By the time they arrived, there were already a dozen buggies and sleighs lined up alongside the building. They piled out with the feeling of excitement. Lizzie was the first to spot Clara and her family.

Together, they all entered the school. A hum of voices filled the building. The floor was the simple wide planking, scuffed and covered with puddles of melting snow from the shoes of the visitors. The student desks had all been pushed to line the walls while rows of backless benches had been arranged down the center of the room to accommodate the family and friends of the scholars who would be performing. Light poured in from the windows along both sides of the single room inside. A large blackboard covered two-thirds of the front wall. Above it, student artwork depicting the nativity had been hung. The childish drawings ranged from simple stick figures done by the first graders to detailed scenes drawn by some of the older students.

Squarely in the middle of the front sat a large stove radiating heat from the coal fire. Slightly off to one side sat the teacher's desk. Books and stacks of papers were arranged neatly on the shelves behind it. To the other side was a small elevated platform that served as a stage. Blankets hung over a wire served as the curtain. Excited children's voices could be heard from behind it. Greta and her family found their places on the wooden benches that had been set up for the spectators.

When the teacher stepped out from behind the makeshift curtain, a hush soon fell over the room. "Good afternoon, and welcome to our Christmas program. I am Melinda Miller. This is my first year teaching at Walnut Valley School. It has been a wonderful experience. My scholars have worked hard on a program for you this evening. To get us started, Joy Mast will recite a poem that she wrote herself."

Joy, a young girl with Down syndrome, came out from behind the curtain. She was dressed as a shepherdess, complete with shepherd's crook. She waved to everyone, came down off the stage to give someone in the front row a hug and then went back to her spot. In a booming voice she read a poem about the shepherds waiting in the fields on Christmas Eve. It didn't all rhyme, but the message was clearly one from her heart.

Marianne leaned toward Greta and whispered, "Why does she look so funny?"

Greta smiled and whispered back, "Because God made her a very special person."

During the next hour, they were entertained by scholars who recited poetry, performed two small plays and sang a dozen Christmas carols, some in English, and some in the traditional German.

As she watched the children, the peace of the season began to seep into Greta's heart. She was actually sorry her uncle wasn't here to enjoy the program. If she had only one Christmas left on earth, this was the way she would want to celebrate it. Surrounded by friends and family and watching the next generation of her community show their love of God in their joyful voices.

She shared a glance with Toby as a new thought sent a surge of heat to her cheeks. Would they one day watch their own children preform in a Christmas pageant?

Chapter Twenty-Six

When the presentation drew to a close, Greta followed the crowd outside where it divided into groups of family and friends happy to see each other and visit for a while before heading home.

Joy Mast came running up to Marianne. "Hi. I'm Joy. Merry Christmas. Did you like my poem? My new mom helped me write it. What's your name?"

"Marianne."

"We can be friends now." Joy threw her arms around Marianne and hugged her.

Stepping back, she pointed to Marianne's neck. "You got hurt. I'm sorry. Does it hurt?"

Marianne covered it with her hand. "Not much anymore."

"That's good. I mean *goot*. Come meet my other friends. Oh, look, there is Dr. White. He says I have Up syndrome, not Down syndrome, because I am always happy and not sad. I like him."

She waved. Dr. White, who was standing with his grandson Philip and Philip's wife, Amber, waved back. Joy's father, Caleb Mast, was standing with them. The group came toward Greta and her family.

Caleb held out his hand to Toby. "I hope my daughter didn't upset your sister. Joy can be a little overwhelming, but she means well."

Greta could tell Toby was keeping a watchful eye on Marianne, but he seemed content to let her find her way with the other children. As Greta had suspected, they were welcoming and ignored her self-conscious efforts to hide her scars.

Amber, who was the local nurse-midwife, gave Lizzie a hug. "You look good. I think pregnancy has finally started to agree with you."

"That's because I can eat like a horse now without morning sickness. Amber, this is Toby Yoder and the little girl with him is his sister, Marianne. They were on their way to Pennsylvania and got stuck at our place during the storm."

"How fortunate for you," Philip said. "Naomi is one of the best cooks in the county. It was a sad day for the Wadler Inn and the Shoofly Pie Café when she gave up her spatula and married Woolly Joe. Naomi, you are going to teach your daughter how to make your special scrumptious shoofly pie, aren't you?"

"Maybe someday. For now, I just like hearing how much folks miss my cooking."

Amber turned to Greta. "Lizzie told me that you were bringing your uncle back from Fort Wayne, Indiana, to stay with you because he had open heart surgery. How is he doing?"

"I'm not sure. He has severe attacks of chest pain."

"Angina?" Philip said.

"The discharge nurse called it unstable angina. The pills they gave him seem to help. He puts one under his tongue. If it doesn't help right away, he takes a second one. I've never seen him take more than two, but I'm worried that I will find him unconscious. Then what do I do?"

"They teach us to think ABC," Amber said. "Check A, is his airway open? Then B, is he breathing, and C for cardiac, which means to check if he has a pulse."

"How do I check that?"

"The easiest way is to press your fingers to the side of his throat. You should feel a steady beat under your fingertips. Check mine." Amber lifted her chin.

Feeling a little foolish, Greta did. Amber was right. It was easy to feel the beat. "If I find A, B and C, then what?"

"If he is still unconscious, you can call for an ambulance," Philip said.

Greta folded her arms over her chest. "He does not wish to go back to the hospital."

"Then you honor his wishes," Dr. White said.

"*Danki.* That is what I will do." Greta smiled at the older man's understanding.

Amber laid a hand on Greta's arm and tugged her away from the group. When they were out of earshot, she said, "I was wondering if you could help me with something, Greta?"

"Anything that's within my power. What do you need?"

"The other day, I saw a young Amish woman in the clinic. She thought that her husband might be abusive. She wasn't sure. She grew up in a very strict family. She wasn't sure if her husband's actions were abusive or simply discipline. I have worked among the Amish for many years as a midwife and I have rarely seen outright abuse. But one case is one too many. Clara has told me about the way your uncle treated all of you. She mentioned that you are interested in pursuing a career in counseling."

"I am." Or she had been until Toby arrived in her life. She couldn't possibly go on with her education if she had plans to become an Amish wife. Although she knew she was getting the cart before the horse, she couldn't help but dream about the possibility.

"My husband and I have talked it over, and we want to start an abuse education campaign among the Amish," Amber said.

Intrigued, Greta asked, "How would you do this?"

Amber's face grew animated. "We want to run informational articles in the newspaper and in the Amish monthly magazine. We already have a column called 'Asked the Doctor,' so that won't be hard. What will be hard is getting the women to talk to us."

"So how can I help?"

"We need someone who is Amish, someone who understands what abuse is, to be available to talk to these women, or children, if they come forward with questions."

It made sense. Few women would openly admit such a thing. "Have you talked to the bishops in this area about this?"

"I have talked to Bishop Zook and several of the bishops from other congregations. Some are on board with this. Some are not. I truly think it's a lack of education about the issue that prevents them from making a decision in our favor. Hence the articles in the newspaper."

The Amish newspaper and magazine were read by Amish people all across the nation. Greta began to share some of Amber's excitement. "I think you are onto something."

"Thank you. I understand that Bishop Zook and other bishops are reluctant to interfere between a husband and wife, but if they are willing to listen to what my husband and I have to say, we may help any number of women and men. When Bishop Zook counsels couples, he wants to do the right thing. However, Philip and I are outsiders. It doesn't matter how long we've lived in this community, we're not Amish. If we could assure the bishop and others that we have an Amish woman willing to be our helper, that might ease their minds. Are you interested?"

"I'm more than interested." A chance to do what she wanted without leaving her Amish faith seemed almost too good to be true. What would Toby think of her decision? Would it change things between them?

Amber grinned. "I'm so glad."

"I do have one question?"

"We would pay you a salary."

"That isn't my question. The young woman who came to see you, was it someone I know?"

"I don't think so. Her family was not from this area."

"Was her husband being abusive?"

"I believe that he was."

"We can educate people, but can we change them?"

"With God's help, anything is possible. If we get the bishops on board, then I believe we will begin to see changes in what is acceptable behavior."

"So when do we start?" Greta asked.

"Come by the office anytime after the first of the year. Our first article is scheduled to run in the newspaper the day after New Year's. I'm sending an invitation to all the area bishops to meet with us on the morning of January sixth. I know it's a holiday for the Amish, but that way none of them will have to miss work. If you could come to that meeting, it would be awesome."

"Do you really think it can make a difference?" Greta tried to quell her growing elation.

"I don't know, but I do know this. Nothing will change if we don't try."

"I will come to your meeting. If Bishop Zook says this is acceptable, I will be happy to work with you."

"And if he believes it is not acceptable?"

"He will. I know he will. This is where the Lord has been leading me. I feel it."

Toby sensed Greta's excitement the moment she returned to his side. "What's up?"

"Amber said they want to start an abuse-education program for the Amish. They want me to be the go-between for Amish women who don't feel comfortable talking to outsiders."

"Can you do it? Can you listen to others who have been hurt the way you were and help them forgive the person who hurt them?"

"It's not just about forgiveness. It's about making men and women aware of what is right and what is wrong. I have felt called to help abuse victims ever since I arrived at my grandfather's home. I saw then that living in fear isn't normal. It isn't how God wants His children to live. If I can help others without leaving the community I love, it will truly be an answer to my prayers."

Toby understood and respected her passion, but he knew that what she wanted was only half the battle she faced. "You say it's not about forgiveness, but for us it is. We believe it must be the first step and not the last one. Have you forgiven your uncle?"

She looked away. "I'm trying. Where is Marianne?"

He allowed her to change the subject although they would go back to it one day soon. "She's on the swing set with Joy. They seem to be getting along really well."

"I knew she would find acceptance here. Have you told her that you are staying?"

"Not yet. She has her heart set on going back to Pennsylvania. I have my heart set on staying here." His heart was standing in front of him, her cheeks flushed, her eyes bright at the prospect of helping others. He loved her more than he thought it was possible to love anyone.

"You will have to tell her soon. Arles's van will be repaired in a few days."

"I know. I haven't found the right time." He wasn't sure how Marianne would react. She had suffered so much. If she refused to stay here, he would have no choice but to leave, too. He didn't want to think about that possibility. He couldn't put his happiness before hers.

"You should take her home to Pennsylvania and return when she is settled."

Had he been mistaken? He thought Greta realized how important his sister's well-being was to him. "I can't leave her there. I can't. After all that has happened to her, I have to take care of her. I can't dump her on someone else and expect to live with myself."

"I wasn't suggesting that."

"It sounded a little bit like you were."

"Please, let's not fight. It's Christmas Eve."

"I'm sorry. I want so much for Marianne to be happy here. To want to stay."

"I know you do and she will be, but you can't keep her in the dark much longer."

"Okay. We can tell her tomorrow, on Christmas morning. You and me together. What you think?"

She smiled and his chest filled with happiness. "I think it's a wonderful idea."

As they rode home in the sleigh with her family that evening, Toby held Greta's hand beneath the quilt again and refused to consider it might be for the last time. Marianne was growing to love Greta and her family. She would be happy that he wanted to settle here.

She had to be.

Please, Lord, let it be Your will.

Chapter Twenty-Seven

Screams woke Greta. She sat bolt upright in the darkness. She was in her bed, but this wasn't a dream. The smell of heavy smoke filled her nostrils. She grabbed Betsy. "Get up. There's a fire. Wake everyone."

Throwing back the covers, Greta raced downstairs toward the screaming. Marianne stood in the doorway to Morris's bedroom with the cat in her arms. Beyond her, Greta saw flames leaping up the bedspread from a fallen lamp.

She grabbed Marianne by the shoulders. "Get back. Get your brother."

The child's stood frozen in place. Holding the sleeve of her robe over her face, Greta plunged into the room rapidly filling with smoke. "*Onkel,* can you hear me? Where are you?"

She heard a moan and saw his foot protruding from the other side of the bed. Grabbing a quilt off a nearby chair, she tossed it over the flames to smother them. It choked off a portion of the fire, but not all of it. The smoldering mattress poured black smoke into the air. Even with her mouth covered, it was choking her. She dropped to her knees and crawled toward her uncle.

"Greta?" She heard Toby shouting for her.

"Here!" She looked back and saw the light from the lantern in his hand. "Get Marianne and the others out. I've got to help my uncle."

"I'll be back for you." He picked up his sister and vanished from the doorway.

Greta's eyes were watering so hard she could barely see, but it was easier to breathe near the floor. She kept crawling until her hand touched her uncle's leg. She took hold of his feet and tried to move him, but she couldn't. She needed better leverage. Taking a deep breath, she stood and pulled with all her might.

He moved a little. Inch by inch, she pulled him away from the bed toward the door. Twice she had to drop to the floor to get a breath. Her lungs were burning. The third time she stood up, she felt someone beside her.

"I've got him. Go!" Toby shouted in her ear.

"I must find his medicine." She knew Morris kept his pills on his nightstand. Groping her way to the wall, she located the vial, gripped it tightly and staggered out of the room toward the kitchen, still half blinded by the smoke. Carl and her grandfather were wetting towels and blankets at the sink and wrapping wet clothes over their faces. They raced past her as she lurched toward the front door, coughing and gagging. She opened it, but her strength deserted her. She sagged against the doorjamb, unable to go on. Toby was right behind her. He had her uncle slung over his shoulder. He wrapped his free arm around her and half carried her outside.

Naomi, Lizzie, Betsy and Marianne were gathered on the sidewalk, huddling together in the bone-chilling cold with quilts over their shoulders. Betsy put an arm around Greta's waist to help her stand.

Lizzie pointed toward the barn. "Carl said we should go down to the lambing shed and wait there. It has a propane heater and there is a cot for Morris. How is he?"

"Alive," Toby said. He headed across the snow-covered ground.

Barefoot, Greta followed and prayed for her uncle as the cold bit deep into her feet. The straw on the lambing shed floor was a blessed relief when she reached it.

Naomi quickly pulled a small army cot out from under a stack of burlap bags and set it up near the stove. Betsy located a pair of battery-powered lamps and turned them on. Lizzie lit the heater. Almost instantly, warmth began to push back the chill of the room.

Toby laid Morris down and took a step back. "I need to help the men."

"Go, we're fine," Naomi assured him.

Marianne launched herself across the small room and threw her arms around him. "Don't leave me."

He dropped to his knees and held her away from him. "I have to help Carl and Joe. I'll be back as soon as I can. I promise. Stay with Greta."

Greta pulled the child away. She read the pain in his eyes, but he rushed out the door leaving Marianne screaming his name. Naomi led the girl to the heater and wrapped a quilt around her. "Don't fret. Your brother is a brave fellow and he loves you. He'll be back as soon as he can. Pray for him and trust God to keep him safe."

Marianne curled into a ball, rocking back and forth as she wept. Greta didn't know if she heard Naomi's words or not.

Greta moved to kneel beside Morris. She tucked the covers around his shoulders. His eyes fluttered, but he didn't open them. She checked his pulse as Amber White had taught her to do and found it erratic. She opened the pill bottle still clutched in her hand and forced a small white tablet under his tongue.

A shiver racked her body. She sat back on her heels and waited. Naomi, Lizzie and Betsy stood in the doorway. Their gazes were fixed on the house as they waited for the men to reappear.

"I don't see flames," Betsy said. Her breath rose in white puffs.

"Where are they?" Lizzie wrapped her arms across her middle.

Betsy bit her thumbnail as she gazed outside. "The smoke was so thick, maybe they've been overcome. I'm going to go check on them."

"You will do nothing of the kind," Naomi said firmly. "They know we are safe. Having one of us run back into danger will only make their job more difficult. We stay here, and we pray."

Like all of them, Naomi was bareheaded. She lifted the quilt from her shoulders and draped it over her hair. Everyone did the same. Their faith required them to cover their heads when praying.

She bowed her head. "Heavenly father, deliver our brave men from danger. Keep them safe, and return them to us unharmed. If it be Your will, spare our home and our belongings. Help us bear this trial with the knowledge that all we have comes to us by Your grace alone. We ask this through Jesus Christ our Lord, amen."

Please let Toby be safe. With the rest of her sisters, Greta echoed, "Amen."

Betsy pointed. "I see someone coming."

Greta rose and hurried to the door to look out. "Who is it?"

Shaking her head, Betsy said, "I can't tell. It's too dark." She held her lamp higher.

It wasn't until the figure reached the circle of light that they could see it was Joseph. Naomi rushed to wrap her arms around him. He kissed her forehead and patted her back. He looked at his granddaughters. "The fire is out, but part of the wall has come down. The place is filled with smoke. You might as well make yourselves comfortable out here for the night."

"Where is Carl?" Lizzie asked with a quiver in her voice.

"He and Toby are dragging the burnt bedding out back. They will be here shortly."

"God be praised," Naomi said.

"He was watching out for us tonight. Thanks to Marianne, we were all warned in time."

The child was still huddled by the heater. Greta sat down beside her and wrapped her arms around her. "Did you hear what my grandfather said? We were all saved because of you. I know this was terribly frightening, but it's over."

Marianne looked up. There were tear tracks through the soot on her face. "Christmas jumped on me and woke me up. I followed her downstairs, and I saw Morris fall and drop the lamp. I was so scared. I grabbed Christmas, but I couldn't run. Where is my brother?"

"He will be back soon."

Greta heard a moan from her uncle, and she moved to kneel beside his cot. "*Onkel* Morris, can you hear me?"

He moaned again.

"Do you need another pill? I have them right here."

He nodded and opened his mouth. She quickly placed one under his tongue. After a few moments, the furrows of pain in his brow began to ease.

"It must make you happy to see me suffer," he managed to mutter.

She sat back on her heels as the truth struck her harder than he ever had. "I can't believe I'm saying this, but it doesn't."

"You hate me. You've always hated me." His voice grew stronger.

"I don't. I did once, but not anymore. I forgive you."

Matt. 5: 43-45

In that instant, she was free of all the bitterness she had carried in her heart for so long. Her soul wanted to sing with joy.

"You should have let me die."

She tucked the blanket around his shoulders. "God makes that decision. I don't get to make it, and you don't get to make it. When He calls you home, nothing I do or say will make a difference."

Morris drew a deeper breath. "Help me sit up."

"I think you should take it easy for a few minutes."

"All right. I might rest a moment longer."

"Take as long as you need."

"Why are you being kind to me?"

"Because our Lord commands it. We are to love those that despise us and care for those who persecute us. Matthew 5:43–45."

He closed his eyes and recited, "'Ye have heard that it hath been said, Thou shalt love thy neighbour, and hate thine enemy.'"

She continued when he stopped. "'But I say unto you, Love your enemies, bless them that curse you, do good to them that hate you, and pray for them which despitefully use you, and persecute you; That ye may be the children of your Father which is in heaven: for he maketh his sun to rise on the evil and on the good, and sendeth rain on the just and on the unjust.'"

"I know the words."

"It is not enough to know the words, *Onkel.* We must live them."

Morris coughed harshly. Greta gave him a sip of water and helped him to lie back. "Rest now."

"I will have all the rest I need when I'm dead."

"Well, don't make me dig a grave in the frozen ground. Have the decency to wait until spring."

He started cackling. "You sound so much like your mother."

"I'm not at all like her. Lizzie is a spitting image of her."

"Lizzie may look like her, but you have that special something that she had. I was in love with her, you know."

"You were in love with our mother?" Greta tried to hide her shock.

"Hard to believe, isn't it."

"Did she…" Greta's voice trailed away.

"Did she feel the same? *Nee*. She couldn't abide me. I had to watch her marry my brother. He didn't deserve her. She found that out eventually. Do you know how hard it was to watch them together? Day after day, year after year, he held the woman who should have been mine. I came to hate them both."

"But you married, too."

"Yes, I married, but I never loved my wife. She knew it. Your mother knew it. My brother had children and I had none. My father was right. Only the strong can survive in this world."

"That is why we must depend on the Lord to hold us up. He is our strength and our salvation."

"I hope that's true. I guess I will find out soon enough."

"You say you never had children, but you had us. Before *Mamm* died, she wanted you to take care of us. That must have meant that she cared for you, respected you."

"As your mother lay dying, she said, 'Send the children to my father. He will give them a loving home.' Even at the end, she couldn't turn to me for help."

"But you told us that she wanted us to stay with you. You wrote to my grandfather and told him his only daughter wanted nothing to do with him."

"Now you know the truth. I am a bitter and vengeful man. Everything I loved was taken away from me. I did my best to make you strong women. You might not think that, but that was my goal. Only the strong prosper."

"I will tell you what you are. You are an old, sick man, who has no one to love and no one to love him. But your life is not over yet. You have a chance to admit your faults and ask God's forgiveness. It is never too late."

"Do you really think He can forgive the likes of me?"

"I have forgiven you. My sisters have forgiven you. God is so much greater than we are. How can you doubt His capacity to forgive? The only thing in doubt is your ability to repent. All you have to do is tell Him you are sorry. Three simple words. Father, I'm sorry. It's Christmas, *Onkel*. This night God sent His only Son to bring us salvation. What better night to honor that gift by accepting it into your heart."

Greta heard Marianne's glad cry and looked toward the door. Toby, his pajamas covered in soot, was truly the most beautiful sight she had ever seen. In that instant, she knew she loved him. She would love him all her life.

Marianne dropped the cat and flew to him. Toby lifted his sister in his arms and came to stand beside the cot.

Greta wanted to throw herself into his arms, too. She wanted to share with him the joy that forgiveness had unleashed in her heart. He would understand the wonder of it and rejoice with her. Instead, she stayed where she was and silently thanked God for safely delivering him and all her family.

"Are you all right, sir?" he asked, looking down at Morris.

"I'm better now. Help me to my feet."

"You should rest. All of you should get what rest you can. It will be daylight before we can assess the damage to the house. It will be safer if we all stay here."

Marianne lifted her tear-stained face from his shoulder. "Take me home now, Toby. I don't want to stay here anymore. I want *Aenti* Linda. I want my family. I want to go home. Please take me home. Please, please, let's go home."

He patted Marianne's back, but his gaze locked with Greta's. "I will, honey. I'll take you home as soon as I can."

"Promise?"

He held her tight, but his eyes never left Greta's face. "I promise."

Greta turned away so he couldn't see that her heart was breaking into little pieces. He wouldn't be staying. He would take his sister home, and Greta would never see them again. Tears sprang to her eyes, but she willed them away. She understood why he had to leave, but that didn't lessen her pain.

Carl and Joseph opened several bales of hay and shook the tightly packed leaves into a bedding of sorts. The women spread their quilts on top of the hay and everyone settled in to wait out the night.

Greta lay down, too, and turned on her side away from the others. Sorrow closed her throat and forced a single silent tear to slip out. How could she bear losing Toby and Marianne? They had become the breath of joy in her life.

Was this God's will for them?

Although she didn't think she could sleep with the weight of her sorrow pressing down on her chest, Greta finally dozed off. She jerked awake to see faint pink light beyond the frost-coated windowpane.

She rolled over and saw Toby watching her from his quilt. Marianne lay sleeping between them. "Merry Christmas," he said quietly.

"Merry Christmas," Greta replied without smiling. She knew this was goodbye. "Our journey together has ended."

"We still have today," he said.

Tears pricked her eyes. It wouldn't be enough. She blinked them away. "Last night I found the forgiveness that has eluded me. I wanted you to know."

Tenderness filled his eyes. "I'm glad for you. That is the best Christmas gift of all."

It was, but she was a selfish woman. She wanted one more gift. She wanted him to stay with her. Always.

Chapter Twenty-Eight

The Shetler farm became a beehive of activity by mid-afternoon on Christmas Day. Word of the fire spread and dozens of neighbors and friends arrived by buggy, wagon and sleigh to offer assistance and bring portions of their Christmas dinners to share with the family. The day was cold, but the clothesline was soon full of blue dresses, aprons, work pants, shirts and bedding. Everything reeked of smoke and soot.

Greta never found a stolen moment alone with Toby. Marianne clung to him, fretting if he was out of her sight for even a minute. Speaking glances were all they were able to share. It was the worst day of Greta's life, but she kept a smile on her face. She wouldn't ruin Christmas for her family by dissolving into tears.

Perhaps it was best that they weren't alone. It would only make their parting that much more painful. If that were even possible.

Morris recovered slowly, but he was able to be up and around by evening when the family was alone once more and gathered round the kitchen table. He rose to his feet and in a halting and emotion-filled voice, he begged the forgiveness of each of his family in turn, saving Joe for last.

Morris faced his host and cleared his throat. "Joseph Shetler, I have harmed you the most of all. I kept from you your beloved daughter's last words and wrote instead a letter I knew would pain you. Your daughter loved you. As she lay dying, she begged me to send her daughters to you. She knew you give them a loving home. Instead, I wrote to you of her death and led you to believe she wanted you to have nothing to do with her children. I was cruel and caused you many years of loneliness and grief. It was wrong and I beg your forgiveness now."

Her grandfather stood face-to-face with Morris. He wiped his eyes and then gave Morris a kiss upon his cheek. "I forgive you."

Greta glanced around the table. All of her sisters and Naomi had tears in their eyes. She looked at Toby and found he was watching her. He smiled at her. He was happy for her family, but she read the sadness underneath.

Betsy leaned over and linked her arm with Greta. "I was wrong. *Onkel* Morris has not ruined our Christmas. He has made this one the best one of all."

Arles, with his newly repaired van, was waiting in the yard the next morning. Greta stood beside Toby on the porch, determined not to cry. She knew this was hard enough for him without her making it harder. Marianne had gone to say goodbye to Morris.

Toby shook his head. "Greta, you know I want to stay, don't you?"

"I know."

"If it was just me, it would be different."

"Marianne needs you."

I need you, too.

The words were shouting inside her brain, but she kept silent.

"Marianne isn't strong enough yet. She needs her family around her. She needs time to heal."

Greta cupped his face with her hand. "You need time to heal, too."

He looked down. "I have made so many bad decisions. I can't make another bad decision for her."

"I understand." Greta withdrew her hand.

"You are a wonderful person. You are bright and kind. You know how to bring out the best in people. You have a gift. I want you to know that I will always be grateful for what you have done for Marianne. She has come so far because of you."

The girl they spoke of came out of the house carrying Christmas over her arm. She was smiling, eager to go home and see the people she loved. "Goodbye, Greta. You will write like you promised, won't you?"

Greta knelt in front of her. "I will. You must promise me something in return."

"Sure."

Greta looked up at Toby. "You must take very good care of your special brother."

Marianne smiled as she slipped her hand inside Toby's. "I can do that."

Toby drew a ragged breath. "Did you say goodbye to *Onkel* Morris?"

"I did. Can we go now?"

Toby nodded. "*Ja,* it's time to go. Goodbye, Greta Barkman. May God bless and keep you."

"And you, as well, Toby Yoder."

"Perhaps our paths will cross again someday."

She caught the glint of tears in his eyes. "I hope so. I do truly hope so. You and Marianne will always be welcome."

He and his sister walked away and got into the van. When they drove out of the yard, Greta ran in the house, up the stairs and into her room. She threw herself down on her bed and wept her heart out.

* * *

A week later, Toby stood at his aunt's living room window and watched the children building a snowman in the front yard. Marianne and her cousins were rolling enormous balls of snow to stack. He could imagine Greta among them, enjoying the outing. What was she doing this afternoon? Was she missing him at all?

Please, Lord, let her be happy.

His aunt came to stand beside him. "I told you that Marianne would come out of her shell once she returned to her family. She has only been here a week and look how she has blossomed. She is improving every day. It does my heart good to see her happy."

"Me, too."

"Unfortunately, I can't say the same thing about you. You are not happy."

He knew better than to pretend he didn't understand what she was talking about. His aunt was every bit as perceptive as Greta. "I'm trying not to let it show, but I miss Greta terribly."

"You do a good job of keeping it hidden from Marianne."

"*Goot.* That's the way I want it."

"She's okay here. If you wanted to go visit a friend, Marianne will understand."

"I don't think she's ready for that."

"Don't you mean that you aren't ready for that? Toby, you can't live your life for her alone. God must be at the center of your life. You must seek to do His will, not your sister's will."

"But what if taking care of Marianne is what God wants of me? How do I know I'm not being selfish again when I think about my own future?"

"That's where prayer comes in. Listen with your heart and you will find God's answer for you."

"I'm not sure I know how to do that."

"What was the last thing you asked of Him?"

"I asked him to let her be happy."

His aunt gestured toward the window. He saw Marianne in the midst of a snowball fight, laughing and chasing after her cousin with a handful of snow. "I think God has answered that prayer."

"I wasn't thinking of Marianne at that moment."

"Then perhaps that was your heart speaking to you."

After his aunt left the room, he turned away from the window and took up the wooden box he had been carving. Picking up a narrow chisel, he began to deepen the outline of the design he had chosen. It was a picture of a cat gazing out a window. A woman's hand rested on the cat's head.

Greta had such capable hands. He remembered how small and yet how strong they had felt when he'd held them on their sleigh ride. He remembered the way his heart skipped a beat when she touched his face. He put his tool aside and traced the outline of her hand with his fingers.

He would never forget the sorrow in her eyes the day he left. It haunted his dreams.

"That looks like Christmas."

He glanced up to find Marianne studying his work. "I didn't hear you come in. Are you okay?"

"I'm fine. My toes were getting cold so I decided to warm them up. Is that my hand on Christmas's head?

"I guess it could be."

"It's Greta's hand, isn't it? I miss her, don't you?"

"A little." He began working again, carving small slivers of wood with each pass of his chisel.

"She misses you, too."

"And how do you know that?"

"She said so in her letter."

His gaze snapped to his sister's face. "You've had a letter from Greta already?"

"Yup."

"What did she say? How is she? Did she mention me?"

"She said she hopes we are happy here."

Of course that was what she would write. What else could she say? He looked back at his work. "You must be sure and tell her that we're doing fine. You are happy, aren't you?"

She bit the corner of her lip and turned away. "Most of the time. Sometimes I'm sad because I miss *Mamm* and *Daed. Aenti* Linda is a lot like *Mamm,* but she isn't *Mamm.*"

"You like having your cousins to play with, I know you do."

"Sure I do. I told Greta I was happy in my letter to her, but I told her that you were sad a lot."

He put down his tools and took his sister's hands. He pulled her around so that she was facing him. "I'm sorry if you think I'm sad. I'm not. I am happy if you are happy."

"But you're not cheerful the way you were when we were staying with Greta's family. You used to laugh. You don't laugh now."

He couldn't lie to her. He picked up his tools again. "I enjoyed their company. They were very kind to us."

"*Onkel* Morris wrote that Greta is very sad now. He says she never smiles anymore. He says she misses me and that you and I are the only ones who can cheer her up. Do you think we can go back and see them sometime soon?"

"Maybe someday." He hated hearing Greta was sad. Their love wasn't meant to be. He had to accept that.

"Will you be sad until then?"

He smiled brightly although it wasn't from the heart. "I will not be sad at all."

He was no good at lying. Marianne saw right through him. She sighed and walked over to the window. The cat was sitting on the ledge watching the activity outside. Marianne stroked the animal's head. "Christmas is sad, too. She misses *Onkel* Morris. I think she is really his cat."

"She's your cat."

"I thought so, but she isn't. She has to go back. *Onkel* Morris needs her to watch over him until his heart is better. It's important."

"I'm sure we can find a way to get her back to Ohio."

Marianne whirled around and smiled. "We can take her."

He thought his aunt had gone, but she had come back into the room and was standing in the doorway behind him. "Toby, I told you that you can leave Marianne with me for as long as she wants to stay. She'll be fine."

"But I want to go visit Greta, too. I miss her. I like it here, I do, *Aenti* Linda, but I miss Greta and Naomi. I miss Joe and Duncan. I miss the sheep, too."

Toby crossed the room to kneel in front of his sister. He placed his hands on her shoulders. "I know you miss them, but you wanted to come here. You can't be in two places at once."

Her bottom lip quivered. "I know."

Two of his aunt's young daughters came in with dolls in their arms. "Marianne, come play school with us."

She started to follow them out of the room, but stopped and looked back. "*Aenti* Linda, would you be sad if I went with Toby to see Greta?"

Her aunt shook her head and smiled in understanding. "*Nee,* I would not be sad. Now that I have seen how happy and well you are, I know God has wonderful things in store for you. Besides, something tells me I will get to meet Greta soon, too."

Marianne grinned. "You'll love her like I do." She ran out of the room after her cousins.

Toby's heart started pounding so hard he thought it would leap out of his chest. "I have nothing to offer Greta.

I don't have a job or a place to live. It isn't fair to Marianne, or to you, to take her away so soon. What if she wants to return here again?"

"What if she doesn't? Take the cat to Morris. See how things go from there."

He raked a hand through his hair as he paced across the room and back. "I don't know."

"What are you afraid of, Toby?"

He stopped and looked at his aunt. "If I go back to Greta, I won't be able to leave her. Not even for my sister."

"How did the meeting go?" Carl asked as he took hold of the pony's bridle. The sun was shining brightly but very little of the snow had melted in the twelve days since Christmas. The countryside remained blanketed under a brilliant and glittering white cover.

Greta stepped down from her cart. Her sisters came hurrying out of the house. She knew they had been watching for her.

"Well?" Betsy demanded.

"What did he say?" Lizzie asked, pressing close.

"Don't keep us in suspense," Clara added.

"Tell us," Betsy and Lizzie said together.

Greta shook her head, but she was glad to share her news. "I will tell you if you all stop talking. It went well. The bishops listened to my story. A majority of them, including Bishop Zook, have agreed to allow Amber and Dr. White to interview and counsel Amish abuse victims if I am with them. I'm going to speak about the project at different churches after their services for the next few months."

"That's wonderful," Clara said, embracing Greta.

"I won't have to leave the Amish to help others who are suffering as we did. God is good," Greta said softly. She was thankful for all the Lord had done for her, but more than anything, she wanted to share her news with Toby. She would have to write, but it wouldn't be the same. She longed to see the joy she knew he would feel at her decision.

Lizzie pulled her shawl tightly across her chest. "Let's go in the house. It's cold out here."

Inside the house, Naomi was busy putting the finishing touches on the meal. The house was filled with the smell of roasting turkey, stuffing and pumpkin pies cooling on the counter. Thanks to the efforts of the entire community, the house was as good as new. There was little evidence that there had ever been a fire. Joe was seated at the table enjoying a cup of coffee and staying out of the way. As she knew they would be, her grandparents were thrilled with her news.

She left the kitchen and went into the living room. Betsy followed her.

"I know it's probably a fruitless question, but where did you put your smile, Greta?"

Greta sighed and turned to look at her little sister. She pointed to her cheek. "It's right here on my face."

"Not the fake smile. It's Old Christmas today. Everyone is here to celebrate with us. Where did you put your real smile?"

"Someone took it to Pennsylvania with him," Morris said walking in from his room.

Greta scowled at him. "You're eavesdropping again."

"How am I supposed to learn anything interesting if I don't listen at keyholes?" The sarcasm was gone. There was only gentle humor in his tone. He could still be sharp, but he tried hard not to be cruel. Greta was grateful for that.

"Did you want something, *Onkel?*" she asked.

"Just to tell you that your belated Christmas gifts are coming down the lane."

"What are you talking about?" Greta moved to look out the living room window. She couldn't believe her eyes. She blinked hard and looked again. Toby and Marianne were walking toward her house.

She started to run outside and then stopped. She turned to look at her uncle. "What have you done?"

"Me? Nothing."

"I don't believe you."

"I wrote a letter to a friend urging her to come and visit. It appears she has answered me. Greta, real love, the kind that lasts through this life and beyond is a rare thing. Don't waste it."

Greta pulled her coat on and walked out to meet Toby. Marianne held Christmas in her arms. When Marianne caught sight of Greta, she put the cat down. Christmas ran past Duncan who lay dozing in the sun and raced up the porch steps. The dog woke with a start and looked around. He spied the cat sitting in front of the screen door and began wagging his tail.

Toby stood with his hands in pockets as Greta embraced Marianne. "I'm so glad to see you, little one."

Marianne wrapped her arms tightly around Greta's neck. "I'm happy to see you. I brought Toby to visit you because he's been sad and Christmas wants to stay with *Onkel* Morris. I've missed you and *Onkel* Morris, too. Can I go see him?"

Greta released her and managed a smile. "He's inside waiting for you, and Clara's children are playing out in the barn. I know they'll want to see you, too."

"Wunderbarr." She ran toward the house.

They had come for a visit and nothing more. Greta finally gained enough control of her emotions to look at Toby. She had missed him so much. He looked so wonderful. "How have you been?"

"Miserable. I had to see you, Greta."

Crossing her arms, Greta stared at her shoes. "Marianne looks good. She must enjoy being with her aunt and cousins."

"She has, but she missed you and your family."

"We've missed her, too." His sister was healing with his family, as he knew she would. He had been right to take her home. Greta was glad she'd had a chance to see that for herself. This time when he left, she could console herself that Marianne was where she belonged.

He gave an exasperated sigh. "I didn't come here for small talk. We started out on a simple short journey together, Greta. That's all it was meant to be."

"And that's all it was." He shouldn't have come back. Their break had been hard, but this was harder. She wanted to throw herself into his arms and sob her heart out.

"Our journey was short, but it was only the start of our journey. Greta, I can't accept a life without you in it. I know we haven't known each other long, but I have never known anyone as well as I know you."

"How can you say that?" She walked away from him.

He caught up with her and stopped in front of her to block her way. "I can say it because it's true. I know how you have struggled to forgive your uncle. I can see how happy you are to be free of that burden. I'm happy for you. I know you are kind, I know you are enormously helpful to others. I know you see helping others as your calling in life. That is a wonderful thing."

"I told you these things. That doesn't mean you know me." She crossed her arms over her chest. If he knew her, he would know her heart was breaking at the thought of watching him leave again.

"Greta, I know your family doesn't always understand you. I know you like the color green. I know you like animals. At this moment, I wish I was a cat with a lopped off ear because you would be trying to heal me. What you can't see is that I'm a man with part of his heart lopped off. I lost a piece of it the moment I walked away from you."

"I'm sorry we hurt each other, but I understand why you had to leave."

"But do you understand why I had to come back? This isn't something a simple bandage will fix. Only your compassion, only your love can begin to fix what's wrong with me."

"You were right to leave with your sister. She needs you. Everyone could see that, even my uncle."

"Yes, I was right to take Marianne back to Pennsylvania, but I was wrong to leave you here without any hope of my return. Without telling you how much you meant to me. Without telling you that I love you. Do you hear me, Greta Barkman? I'm in love with you. I'm not going anywhere until I hear four simple words from you."

She gazed into his eyes and bit the corner of her lip. Would he stay if she asked him to? Would he leave his sister? Did she have the right to ask him to do that? "I don't know what you expect me to say."

"I want you to say, *I love you, Toby,* or *I don't love you.*"

"That's it? That's all I have to say?"

"That's it. So choose."

She spun away. "It isn't that simple.

"It is. It's like a cross-stitching. It looks complicated, but it isn't. Needle in and needle out. *I love you, Toby,* or *I don't love you.*"

Stiffening her spine, she faced him. "I don't love you."

He took a step back, a look of shock on his face. Greta didn't want to hurt him, but he had given her no choice. He would regret choosing her over his sister forever.

"Okay, now I know that you can tell a lie. Why is it so hard to admit the truth? I'm sorry you feel I don't deserve you."

Her mouth dropped open. "I never said you didn't deserve me."

"That's what I heard."

"You heard wrong."

"Then I do deserve you." He rocked back on his heels with a smug grin.

She pressed her fingers to temples. "Stop trying to confuse me."

"I'm not trying to confuse you. Either I don't deserve your love, or I do. I like those words."

She was getting angry. "What words?"

"I do. I like the sound of those words." He stepped forward and took her hands in his. "I would give my life to hear you say those words in front of our friends and family. I deserve to live with the love of a woman God has chosen for me. You deserve to live with the love of a man God has chosen for you. I love you, Greta. We can have a long courtship and get to know each other really well, but we are meant to be together."

"You can't choose me over your sister."

"I have already chosen, but, darling, Marianne wants to live here with you and your family. If she changes her mind, she can go back to *Aenti* Linda. She's strong enough to make that choice. I love you, Greta. You are my choice."

"Oh, Toby, do you really love me?" It was almost too wonderful to accept.

He kissed the back of her hand. "I love everything about you. I love your fingers. I love your cute nose. I love your gorgeous lips. I'm going to find a job and live close by so I can court you as I should. I know I should've asked the first time, but I'm going to ask now. May I kiss you, Greta Barkman?"

Her heart melted into a puddle of joy. "For the record, if you had asked the first time, I would have said yes then, too."

"Did I mention I love your honesty?"

"No, you mentioned that I know how to lie."

"Everyone has faults. I can live with that. Will you say the two words that I'm dying to hear?"

"That depends."

"On what?"

"On whether you ask the question that I've been dying to hear."

"Greta Barkman, do you take this poor lovesick man to love and to obey, for better or for worse, for richer, for poorer, in sickness and in health, until death do us part?" He leaned close until his lips were only a breath away from her ear.

"I do," she whispered.

Greta closed her eyes. His tender kiss took her breath away and sent her soul soaring. God had blessed her in more ways than she could count, but she would spend a lifetime giving thanks for every one of them. Especially for this man.

* * * * *

Dear Reader,

I hope you have enjoyed Greta's journey. The Christmas season led her to discover forgiveness in her heart. That, in turn, made room for Toby's love to come in and grow.

Forgiving those who have harmed us, physically or emotionally, can be very difficult. I struggle with this as much as anyone, but without finding that strength within ourselves we can remain victims and not victors. Abuse is not an easy topic to discuss, and I certainly did not mean to trivialize it in any way when I wrote this book. The recovery for victims and perpetrators is much more complex than I had room to write about here.

If you or someone you know is the victim of abuse, I urge you to seek help. Reaching out can save a life.

I wish you and your families a safe and happy Christmas season. Let the Light of the World shine in your life and in all you do.

Blessings,

Patricia Davids

Questions for Discussion

1. Do you believe the family made the right decision in agreeing to allow Morris to move into their home? Could you do so? Why or why not?

2. Both Greta and Toby are dealing with issues related to their pasts. How do you feel they helped each other?

3. What purpose did you discover for the addition of Christmas the cat to this story?

4. Did you learn anything new about the Amish culture in reading this book?

5. Did you learn anything new about sheep while reading this story?

6. What was the most touching moment in this book for you and why?

7. Why do you think Greta and Toby found such an instant attraction to each other? Do you believe in love at first sight?

8. How can we, as Christians, help prevent child abuse in our society? Is education the answer?

COMING NEXT MONTH FROM
Love Inspired®

Available December 16, 2014

HER COWBOY HERO
Refuge Ranch • by Carolyne Aarsen

When rodeo cowboy Tanner Fortier ropes ex-fiancée Keira Bannister
into fixing his riding saddle, the reunited couple just might have a chance
to repair their lost love.

SMALL-TOWN FIREMAN
Gordon Falls • by Allie Pleiter

Karla Kennedy is eager to leave Gordon Falls, but working with hunky
fireman Dylan MacDonald on the firehouse anniversary celebration has
this city girl rethinking her small-town future.

SECOND CHANCE REUNION
Village of Hope • by Merrillee Whren

After a troubled past, Annie Payton is on the road to recovery. Now she
must convince her ex-husband she's worthy of his forgiveness—and a
second chance at love.

LAKESIDE REDEMPTION
by Lisa Jordan

Zoe James returns home to Shelby Lake for a fresh start—not romance. So
when she starts to fall for ex-cop Caleb Sullivan, will she have the courage
to accept a second chance at happily-ever-after?

HEART OF A SOLDIER
Belle Calhoune

Soldier Dylan Hart can't wait to surprise pen-pal Holly Lynch in her
hometown. But when he discovers that sweet Holly has kept a big secret
from him, can their budding romance survive?

THE RANCHER'S CITY GIRL
Patricia Johns

Cory Stone's determined to build a relationship with his estranged father,
but when he invites the ill man to join him at his ranch, Cory never expects
to find love with his dad's nurse.

LICNM1214

REQUEST YOUR FREE BOOKS!

2 FREE INSPIRATIONAL NOVELS
PLUS 2
FREE
MYSTERY GIFTS

Love Inspired

LI13R

Keira wished she could keep her hands from trembling as she handled Tanner's saddle. What was wrong with her?

Seeing him again, his brown eyes edged with sooty lashes and framed by the slash of dark brows, the hard planes of his face emphasized by the stubble shadowing his jaw and cheeks, brought back painful memories Keira thought she had put aside.

He looked the same and yet different. Harder. Leaner. He wore his sandy brown hair longer; it brushed the collar of his shirt, giving him reckless look at odds with the Tanner she had once known.

And loved.

She sucked in a rapid breath as she turned over the saddle on the table. Tanner seemed to fill the cramped shop.

Keep your focus on your work, she reminded herself.

"So? What's the verdict?" Tanner asked.

"I don't know if it's worth fixing this," she said, quietly. "It'll be a lot of work."

Tanner sighed. "But can you fix it?"

"I'd need to take it apart to see. If that's the case, two weeks?".

"That's cutting it close," Tanner said. "Is it possible to get it done quicker?"

Keira would have preferred not to work on it at all. It would mean that Tanner would be around more often.

It had taken her years to relegate Tanner to the shadowy recesses of her mind. She didn't know if she could see him more often and maintain any semblance of the hard-won peace she now experienced. Tanner was too connected to memories she had spent hours in prayer trying to bury.

"I'm gonna need it for the National Finals in Vegas in a couple of weeks." Tanner continued.

"I heard you're still doing mechanic work, as well?" She was pleasantly surprised she could chitchat with Tanner, the man who had once held her heart.

"Yup, except last year I bought out the owner. Now I'm the boss, which means I can take off when I want. I took over the shop in Sheridan after a good rodeo run. The same one I started working on before—" He didn't need to finish. Keira knew exactly what "before" was.

Before that summer when she left Tanner and Saddlebank without allowing him the second chance he so desperately wanted. Before that summer when everything changed.

A heavy silence dropped between them as solid as a wall. Keira turned away, burying the memories deep, where they couldn't taunt her.

But Tanner's very presence teased them to the surface.

She looked up at him to tell him she couldn't work on the saddle, but as she did she felt a jolt of awareness as their eyes met. She tried to tear her gaze away, but it was as if the old bond that had once connected them still bound them to each other.

Will Keira agree to fix Tanner's saddle?
Pick up HER COWBOY HERO to find out.
Available January 2015, wherever
Love Inspired® books and ebooks are sold.

SPECIAL EXCERPT FROM

SUSPENSE

SWAT team member Isaac Morrison didn't plan to fall for his best friend's sister. But when Leah Nichols and her son are in trouble, he'll stop at nothing to keep them out of harm's way.

Read on for a sneak peek of
UNDER THE LAWMAN'S PROTECTION
by Laura Scott

"Stay down. I'm going to go make sure there isn't some-one out there."

"Wait!" Leah cried as Isaac was about to open his car door. "Don't go. Stay here with us."

He was torn between two impossible choices. If some-one had shot out the tires on purpose, he couldn't just wait for that person to come finish them off. Nor did he want to leave Leah and Ben here alone.

So far he wasn't doing the greatest job of keeping Hawk's sister and her son safe. If he'd been wearing his bulletproof gear he would be in better shape to go out to investigate.

Isaac peered out the window, trying to see if anyone was out there. Sitting here was making him crazy, so he decided doing something was better than nothing.

"I'm armed, Leah, so don't worry about me. I promise I'll do whatever it takes to keep you and Ben safe."

He could tell she wanted to protest, but she bit her lip and nodded. She pulled her son out of his booster seat

LISEXP1214

and tucked him next to her so that he was protected on either side. Then she curled her body around him. The fact that she would risk herself to protect Ben gave Isaac a funny feeling in the center of his chest.

Leah's actions were humbling. He hadn't been attracted to a woman in a long time, not since his wife had left him.

But this wasn't the time to ruminate over the past. Isaac's ex-wife and son were gone, and nothing in the world would bring them back. So Isaac would do the next best thing—protect Leah and Ben with his life if necessary.

Don't miss
UNDER THE LAWMAN'S PROTECTION
by Laura Scott,
available January 2015 wherever
Love Inspired® Suspense books and ebooks are sold.